RUINED

M. O'KEEFE

CHAPTER ONE

YOU WANT TO know what the rich and powerful do? They go to parties like this one. And on little plates they carry food around that they don't actually eat. In heavy crystal glasses they drink champagne and scotch. Rivers of it. They laugh and whisper and watch each other out of the corners of their eyes.

But really what they do is pretend. That's all. They play pretend in their four-thousand-dollar tuxes and ten-thousand-dollar dresses.

They pretend to care what the person they're talking to is actually saying. They pretend to give a shit about whatever cause to which they're donating money. Or in the case of tonight's party—the marriage of a 20-year-old girl to a 48-year-old man.

They pretend that it's not gross.

My sister Zilla and I played a version of this exact same game that hot summer under the willow tree at the back of our estate. Wearing our mother's nightgowns with thin little straps and lace that fell past our little girl knees, Zilla would hold out a leaf with a worm on it.

"It's a delicacy where I come from," she'd say in a ridiculous accent.

"After you," I'd say, trying to sound like the Queen of England but getting tangled up somewhere in the deep south. And then, because she was fearless, Zilla would pick up that worm, bite it in half, and swallow it down.

"Show me," I'd say, and she'd open her mouth to reveal nothing but her molars poking through the tender pink of her gums. And then she'd dab the corners of her mouth with the leaf, and we'd tip our heads back and fake laugh.

But the fake laughs always turned to real ones. Ones that shook our bellies and made us collapse onto the ground.

That was not going to happen at this party.

"Are you all right?" asked Mrs. . . . *oh, god, what was her name*? She was important, I'd been told that earlier. I'd been told not to forget that this woman in the vast sea of important women at this party, was *important*.

"I'm fine," I said, but there was sweat pooling between my breasts. The sweat had nothing to do with the heat of summer in Upstate New York

2

and everything to do with my life ending while people ate shrimp cocktail.

The harpist in the corner struck up what sounded like the exact same song she'd been playing for the last hour. It was. It was the same song. The harpist was playing a joke on all the assholes at this party.

Oh god, the thought just occurred to me— she thinks I am one of the assholes.

"As I was saying," the important woman said. The diamonds in her ears were the size of pea gravel and could keep Zilla in Belhaven for a month. "The senator has done excellent work for the state in Washington. Everyone here fully supports his tax relief bill."

"I'm sure he appreciates that."

"Tell him, won't you?" she asked, leaning in closer. "I have a nephew graduating Harvard and he's hoping to intern with the senator next year."

Little did Important Woman know, I had no power. Everything about me—from the dress I was wearing to the seven million thread count pillowcase I would lay my head upon tonight— was a loan I was in the process of paying back.

"Sure," I said.

"You must be so excited," Important Woman said. "How that man has managed to stay single is a mystery to me."

"I think I just need to get a breath of fresh air," I said and then rudely, really rudely, just walked away from that important woman.

Whoa.

I was really starting to unravel. Despite being in this house roughly a million times, I couldn't seem to find a door leading to a room I wanted to be in.

There was like . . . a hysterical giggle in my chest. Or a scream? Maybe it was a scream. Or a sob.

All three?

Was that even possible?

I'd wished a million times since all this started that I was more like my sister. Tougher. Stronger. Angrier.

Strong was never a word anyone had applied to me.

I had to get out of the Constantine compound. Now. Three seconds ago.

The champagne glass in my hand was empty, and I handed it to a waiter, not waiting to answer his polite question about having more of the expensive bubbly. If I opened my mouth too wide I was afraid, well, not afraid as much as I was sure, *absolutely sure* that I would ruin not just this night. But everything—the whole spider web keeping my sister and me safe would be torn apart. So I kept my mouth shut as I pushed past Tinsley Constantine.

"Are you all right, Poppy?" Tinsley asked. We weren't close, me and Tinsley. The Constantine children breathed rarified air, and when I was around them, I felt all the arrows of my circumstances. We'd been raised as cousins of a sort, but we all knew that was a lie. Now, since leaving college, I was staying in their pool house. And they never intentionally made me feel bad, but I could tell they didn't like how much their mother cared about me.

And they really didn't love me staying in the pool house.

"I'm fine," I said with what I hoped was a smile. I could see across the room Winston and Perry, Caroline's sons, tracking this conversation. And more eyes were not what I needed. "I just need some air."

They were one hundred percent pitying me and barely hiding it.

I was one hundred percent freaking out and barely hiding it.

The front doors were still open, people walking in and out, and the big veranda would be just as crowded as this ballroom, so I followed a server out the door and through a wood-panelled study full of men in tuxedos.

I didn't look at their faces. In this world, this place, they all looked the same. White, slightly saggy, watery-eyes behind glasses that assessed my worth as I went running past.

In my desperation, I got turned around inside the sprawling mansion and found myself in the small sitting room being used as a bar for the catering staff. The same room where Caroline had changed my life forever—god, was that . . . Christmas? How had my life changed so dramatically in a few months?

"You have to listen to me," Caroline said, sitting next to me on the little settee facing the icy window. The white twinkle lights reflected in her eyes. "This is serious. And this is hard. But you're not a little girl anymore."

"I know," I said. I'd turned 20 in the spring. And now that Dad was dead, I was Zilla's legal guardian. Frankly, I hadn't been a little girl since Mom died. I wasn't sure I'd ever felt like a little girl.

"Your father . . ." Caroline took a deep breath. "There's no money, Poppy."

"For what?" I asked.

"There's no money for you. For school. For Zilla.

You need to sell the house to pay off what he owed."

"Okay," I felt the ground shifting under my feet. "The life insurance—"

"He cashed it out a year ago."

"My college fund?"

"Gone. The money from your mother's estate. All gone. There's nothing, Poppy."

"How will I pay for Zilla—"

"You're going to need to drop out of school, and we need to figure something out."

"You all right, miss?" a server asked while trying to get by me with a tray of empty glasses from the kitchen.

"Bad place to stop," a guy said, lifting his tray of full glasses over my head as he went by.

"I just need . . . fresh air."

"The front—"

"And privacy."

The server nodded once, her no-nonsense ponytail swishing over her dark vest. "Follow me," she said.

Maybe I could get a job as a server with this catering company. She probably made good money. I didn't have any experience serving appetizers on trays, and probably way too much experience eating them. But I could learn. Probably.

We were through the kitchen and down another hall, and finally she pushed open a door to a small brick patio with a few chairs around what looked like a fire pit. I could see the swimming pool beyond. The pool house where I'd been staying since Christmas like some very unwanted guest. The gazebo. Tennis courts. The manicured lawns slipped down over the hills to the shadowed tree line. Fresh air abounded. The sounds of the party were muffled.

I could almost pretend I was far away from it all.

"You should be okay out here," the server said in her neat vest and bow tie. I loved bow ties. Honestly, I was made to be a catering server.

"Thank you so much!" I said, showing way too much enthusiasm for the kindness she'd shown me, but there'd been a real lack of kindness—big or small, in my life in the last year so I always got a little messy around it.

"It's just where the servers smoke, nothing to get excited about," she said with lots of side eye.

The server vanished through the open doorway, and I walked out into the grass, past the edge of the light thrown from the lantern fixture over the door. In the distance was the thick tree line that separated the Constantine land from my parent's old house. When Zilla found out what Dad had done, she burned the house down. That's when we knew the medication wasn't enough. That's when Belhaven happened. When everything changed. What was left of the house after the fire and the willow tree had been bulldozed, the pond filled, the land sold to the Constantine's.

I could run around to the front of the house and get a key from the valet. Any key. Any car. And I could drive away.

Except, you idiot, you don't know how to drive.

I could run. Just . . . run. Even as I thought it, I was slipping out of my shoes. The grass cold and damp and *real* beneath my feet. That was how bad I wanted to escape—my body was committed to action before I'd fully finished the thought. God. I wanted to *RUN*.

Run and do what? Go where? What about Zilla?

The thoughts were chains erupting out of the grass and wrapping around my feet.

Hands in fists, tears in my eyes, I opened my mouth ready to scream. Ready to let all the poison out, no matter who heard me. Let all of them hear me—Important Woman with the earrings, the Constantine children, the server who in another life might be my best friend—I'd go back in there in a minute and smile and thank them. Show them the stupid rock on my finger and blush and laugh, but now, let them stand in those rooms and know they were robbing me. Killing me. Let them—

"Jesus Christ, you okay?" a thick Irish accent asked from the darkness in the corner of the patio, and instead of screaming I kind of squeaked.

Which, honestly, was about right.

CHAPTER TWO

I COULDN'T SEE the man in the shadows. It was nothing but dark out here, and then there was the red flare of a cigarette to my left, and I stepped back. Embarrassed and shaking, I tripped over my shoes. "I didn't think anyone was here. I'll go—"

"Don't," he said.

"Don't . . . what?"

"Don't leave." Just that. And I was getting bossed around plenty in the house behind me, but no one managed to do it so plainly. It was all dressed up in manners. I was wrapped in chains of politeness. I didn't know what it said about my mental health, but I liked the fact that he didn't ask. And he wasn't polite.

This whole situation was fucking me up.

He didn't step forward to introduce himself, and I stepped away from him keeping my name to myself, too.

"You were just about to do the fifty-yard dash

in a ball gown," he said.

"Not . . . really."

"Then you weren't about to scream, neither."

"No." The lie came easy. So quick. Second nature now.

"Bullshit."

"You know, *you* could leave. Give me some privacy."

His low laugh rippled out from the shadows, putting goosebumps up and down my arms. "Could I?"

"It would be polite."

"I'm not much for polite," he said and took another drag of his cigarette. "I like screaming better than running, though. Gets the blood up."

"The blood up?" That sounded very *Braveheart*. Truthfully, I liked it.

"For fightin' and the like."

"I'm not much for fighting," I said, and it was so true, so funny and true and awful all at the same time I had to put a hand over my mouth so a weird laugh/scream thing wouldn't come tearing out of me. And my chance to run was years behind me.

He made some speculative sound in his throat. Which could be agreement or disagreement or some kind of mix of the two, and it hardly mattered. He hardly mattered. This moment on the patio hardly mattered.

It was why I was still standing there.

Everything inside, every word I said, every drink I had, every person who looked twice at me—all that mattered. It got rung up someplace and added to the price I had to pay.

And I just needed a minute.

"You all right?" he asked.

Terrified.

"You working the party?" I asked, changing the subject. It was always easier to talk about other people.

"You making small talk with the help?" His brogue was so thick it took me a second to make sure I got the words right.

"If that's what you are, then yes."

"Well, I'm not sure what I am, to be honest with you."

"Yeah, me neither."

"In that dress, sweetheart, you are *not* the help."

I pressed my hands to the skirt of my ball gown, gold embroidery and sequins over blush gossamer netting. I felt naked under all the layers, if I was being honest.

"You look beautiful," he said, like he could see

my doubts.

"Thank you." The compliment bounced off me. When people called my sister beautiful, she cut off all her hair and painted her face. Me? I said thank you and did what they asked of me.

"It came in a box," I said, stupidly. "Like in the movies. A box with a big red bow."

"Proof that you shouldn't be out here with me, Princess," he said.

He was right. One hundred percent. There were people inside who, if they found out what I was doing, would be pissed. But the rest of my life was going to be spent trying to not piss those people off, this might be the very last second I had for myself.

"Are you a Morelli?" I asked.

"A who?"

"A member of the Morelli family."

The worst thing he could be was a Morelli. He could be a murdering son of a bitch, and being a Morelli would still be worse.

This guy wasn't the devil. He was a waiter having a smoke. And I wasn't a Constantine. I wasn't even going to be a Waverly for much longer.

"No, I'm not a Morelli," he said.

"Then we're okay." The night seemed to

breathe. The party sounds faded. The scream in my chest was gone.

We're okay.

"Why are you out here?" he asked.

"There are a lot of answers to that question." I laughed.

"You always go for a run during a party?"

"I do." I nodded. "I'm in training."

"For ball gown racing?"

"Yes, it's a very obscure event. But I'm ranked." I was being ridiculous. The nerves were making me ridiculous, and I was only ever ridiculous with my sister.

"National or international?" Oh, he was playing along. It made me want to cry for missing my sister.

"International, of course."

My feet were cold and naked in the grass, so I put on the shoes.

"What are *you* doing out here?" I asked.

"I haven't been invited inside yet."

"Really?"

"No."

That did make me laugh. I liked this shadow Irishman with the quick wit, and maybe it was the grass I could still feel between my toes or that my world was coming down around me in ways I couldn't stop, but the truth just came out of me.

"Adolescent on-set schizophrenia. That's why I'm here. That's why I'm . . . everything."

It was wild to say that out loud. We never talked about it. We never gave the words air or sound. Or light. They lived in shadows, dark and unsaid. Alone and festering.

From the shadows he held a flask. "Here. You look like you could use a drink."

"I shouldn't," I said. I needed to be clear. Sharp. Tonight was like throwing myself into a sea of piranhas. For the rest of my life.

"Your hands are shaking."

Honestly, I couldn't see him. At all. The glow of that cigarette, the gleam off the flask and the white of his shirt at his wrist. He had nice hands. A jagged scar ran along the side of his thumb down to his wrist.

"What happened?" I asked, and I couldn't believe it myself, but I touched his hand. My fingertip brushed the raised pink skin of the scar. The insanity of that made me light-headed, and I quickly took the flask. I cupped it in my cold shaking fingers like a flame.

"Jumped out a window," he said, flexing his fingers out wide and then curling them into a fist. "My hand got caught on an eaves-shoot. Tore it open, like."

"Why'd you jump out a window?"

"Because someone who wanted to hurt me was coming in the door." He said it like a joke.

I took a sip from the flask. The booze burned down my throat and exploded in warmth in my belly, and I gasped. Another sip and the same effect until I could feel my feet and my fingers. Another sip, and my face was warm. Yep. This was what a person needed for a few minutes before jumping into the pool of piranhas. To feel alive. Warm. Bloody and real.

And another sip, the flask lighter in my hand.

"Slow down there," he said and took the flask from me. His fingers didn't touch mine, but I could still feel the heat of them. "I reckon you haven't eaten."

"That," I said, "is a fair point." When was the last time I'd eaten? Last night? Two days ago? I couldn't remember being hungry or full. It felt like I was very tiny inside of my body.

From the shadows around him came one of the china plates from inside. There was cheese there. Little quiches. Asparagus in prosciutto. "Have something," he offered.

"What else have you got over there?" I joked.

"You probably don't want to know. But if

you're hungry." The plate came closer. I reached for a piece of cheese but in the end didn't touch it. My stomach was in knots.

"No, thank you," I said.

"Suit yourself." The plate disappeared, and I was suddenly ravenous.

"Where are you from?" I asked.

"What makes you think I'm not from here?"

Laughter again. But this time, thanks to the flask, it didn't hurt. It didn't sound half like a scream.

"Something about your voice."

"Northern Ireland."

"Belfast?" That was the only town I knew in Northern Ireland.

"Eventually. Derry, too. I was born in a cow pasture you never heard of."

"How long have you been here?" I asked.

He sighed, and I tried again to see him in the shadows, but they were too dark. Too complete. "Five hours."

"I meant the States."

"So do I. I flew into LaGuardia five hours ago."

"And you're here? At this party?"

"Do you know Caroline Constantine?"

"I do," I said with a laugh. My mom's best

friend and a fairy godmother out of the dark when my dad died. We were in her house right now. I slept in her pool house. The net keeping us safe—she'd created. "Did she bring you?"

"In a sense."

"Wow. Well, welcome." It was comforting a little bit. If Caroline was a friend of his, he was one of the good ones. There were rumors around Bishop's Landing that the Constantines were bad news, but those rumors were mostly started by the Morellis who were actual bad news, so I didn't listen to them. And if this guy was attached to the Constantines, being out here in the dark wasn't nearly so scandalous.

"What about you? Where are you from?"

"Here," I said. "I mean, Bishop's Landing."

Just the thought of it brought it all back, what tonight was supposed to be. What I was supposed to do.

I'd like to jump out a window, I thought, but when he laughed I realized I said it out loud. I stepped back again, further into my shadows. The flask was a mistake. Leaving the party was a mistake. I had to keep my head down and swallow my screams, there was no alternative.

"Well," he said quietly. Carefully. "If what's coming through the door is bad enough, the jumping is not so hard."

"I should go back in," I said, turning towards the door but not moving. I took a deep breath, and I heard the snick of a lighter in the shadows. The acrid smell of a cigarette drifted over my shoulder. I didn't smoke, but I suddenly wanted one with a bone-deep desire.

I could hear the scrape of his shoes as he stood up. I imagined him stretching out of the shadows and into the golden light spilling out from the door. I could feel him closer. Warmth against my back. If I turned, I would see him. And just how badly I wanted to see him was a warning.

This man with his charm and accent and flask—was not for me. Not ever.

My heart pounded against my ribcage, and I didn't turn. Coward to the very end. Or perhaps I was just so used to giving up what I wanted. Even the small things. Especially the small things.

They were all I had left, and I was giving them up one crumb at a time.

"Who is coming through your door?" he asked, and I put a hand over my mouth to stop my sob. "Princess?"

"You going to beat someone up for me?" I asked, my voice wrecked.

"If it would help. Even if it won't."

Who could I set this man against? Which person inside that house if left beaten and bloody would free me from this situation? But even if that door was suddenly open to me . . . would I take it? Would I walk out? Would I leave? Risk poverty? Humiliation? My sister . . .

"I'm fine," I said, straightening my shoulders. "What about you? Maybe I should beat someone up for *you*."

"It doesn't work like that. I'm the one who fixes problems."

"Me too," I said. "I am the one who fixes problems, too."

I turned, thinking I was ready for the sight of him. Or had some kind of expectation about what he might look like. I expected handsome. Smiling and charming. Tall, maybe. I was surrounded by handsome men quite a lot.

But I was not braced for him.

He was beautiful. I mean, like inarguably. It was simply fact. A law of nature. Dark hair. Blue eyes like the sky at noon. Dark scruff along his hard, square chin. He wore a tuxedo with the tie pulled loose. An angel kicked out of heaven for the trouble he caused.

There was blood on the collar of his white shirt. Blood from any number of wounds on his face. A black eye. A split lip. A tiny butterfly bandage over a cut on his cheekbone.

He was beautiful, and he was savage.

"What happened to you?" I whispered.

He touched the cut on his lip. "You should see the other guy."

I stepped forward, drawn by the joke attempt. His eyelashes. The sudden urge to be on a side of kindness. Either side. Any side. Just to experience it however I could. "Who hurt you?"

His eyes snapped to mine, sharp and bright, and my skin prickled. Uncomfortable and aware.

"No one," he said, ice cold despite the blood on his collar. The black eye and split lip. "Not for a long time."

I thought he was joking, and I smiled, but his face was resolute. Calm in its strength. He wasn't joking. He wasn't being sarcastic. He's been beaten, but he was telling me it didn't hurt him.

Like he'd made a choice, and that was that. Pain didn't matter.

"It's that easy?" I whispered. Scared in my belly because it was only there that I could acknowledge that I *knew* what was coming for me was going to hurt.

"No," he said, and his hand, the one with the scar, the one I'd touched, brushed my cheek, his thumb at the edge of my lip. "It's not easy. It's very hard. But it's how you survive."

His thumb pressed against my lip, and I gasped, my lips parting. I could taste the salt of his skin and everything in me screamed to leave. This wasn't just foolish, it was dangerous. For him.

For me. Especially for me.

But I couldn't move. He pressed and pressed until my teeth cut into my lip and it hurt.

It hurt, and he kept pushing.

It hurt, and I stood there. Taking it.

Why was I doing this? Why was he? It felt like a warning and a lesson, and it felt *real*. Like the grass under my feet. Like the booze in my belly. Not at all like the threats inside that house, whispered and insinuated. The pain, the taste of blood and salt from his finger. The look in his eye willing me to stillness.

So. Real.

"Don't let them hurt you," he said.

His words broke the spell and heart pounding, I stepped back, but I didn't leave. Like a fool, I stayed.

He didn't have to be a Morelli to be trouble. Or to get me in trouble.

This man was lethal. And so attractive it hurt.

It actually hurt.

"Who are you?" I asked, licking the blood off my lip. Hoping for a lingering taste of him.

He shook his head. "I am no one."

Someone came to stand in the doorway, breaking up the light, casting a shadow across the stranger's beautiful face. Both of us turned to look.

"Jesus, Princess," my Irishman whispered when he saw who was standing there and he must have realized who I was.

"Poppy?" It was the senator, and I went cold. Tried so hard not to, but head to toe the chill settled over me. "Everything all right?"

"I'm fine," I said and smiled to prove it. He always believed my smiles. Everyone did. They were very good smiles. Or maybe he just didn't care.

"We're about to make the announcement," the senator said, and he summoned me with his fingers. A kind of snapping thing like you'd do with a dog, and I told myself, like I had for a while now, that it wasn't personal. It was actually the opposite of personal. He treated everyone like that. That *that* made me feel better wasn't something I was actually proud of. But I was seeking comfort from any corner.

"I'll be in in a second," I said. I wanted to say goodbye to this stranger. To these quiet moments of rest.

Or maybe I just wanted to pull my leash as taut as possible, to see how far it would stretch.

"Poppy?" The senator smiled when he said my name, but the steel was there. That terrifying sharpness. Turns out my leash didn't stretch far at all.

"You heard her," the Irishman said from the shadows. "She needs a second."

"I'm sorry, who are you?" Jim stepped into the light; he was smiling but it was the razor's edge. Jim was blonde and blue eyed. He wore glasses that made him look smart. He worked out just enough that the suits he wore looked good.

Everything about him inspired comfort and confidence.

Voters loved him.

I'd never been so scared of someone in my life.

"I'm coming," I said, and I stepped into the light with Jim Maywell, the junior senator of New York who was 28 years older than me, and at midnight, we were announcing that I would be his wife.

Jim grabbed my hand too hard. But I expected it, and made my hand as small as I could in his. There was a trick to funneling my fingers, so he couldn't grind the bones together. I'd learned that fast. I wondered if that would be interesting on my application to the catering company.

Experience: eating canapes off trays and mitigating the pain my fiancé wanted to inflict on my body.

We stepped off the small patio into the doorway with the sound of the party filtering through the walls.

Don't do it, I told myself. Don't look. He's not for you. Not ever.

But of course, I couldn't stop myself, and I looked back over my shoulder, but the Irishman was gone.

Nothing was left of him but the taste of blood in my mouth.

CHAPTER THREE

Two years later

THE PHONE RANG once, or barely, maybe. It barely rang, and I grabbed it.

"Zilla?" I tried to keep my voice calm. That's what Dr. Anderson said I should do. Dr. Anderson actually said that it was the most important thing. Staying calm. Being calm. Sounding calm.

"You have a collect call from Belhaven Institution. Do you accept these charges?"

Oh god. Good. Belhaven. My hands shook.

"I do," I said. "Of course."

"I'm fine." My sister's voice, exhausted and thin, was the best thing I'd heard in the seven long days since I'd spoken with her.

I pulled the phone from my ear and covered my mouth, trying to get myself under control.

"Poppy?" My sister pulled me back. "I know you're crying. You can cry."

That was not what Dr. Anderson said, but I

collapsed backwards in the very uncomfortable armchair in the front sitting room. "Are you okay?" I asked her.

"I said I was fine."

"You were gone. You weren't—"

"I checked myself back into Belhaven."

I folded over my legs, a pain in my stomach that was spreading to my chest. I heard from her a week ago and then silence. No answering her cell phone. Emails. Texts. I went by her apartment, and it was empty. Like . . . *empty* empty. And I'd spent the last week sure she'd . . . done something horrible.

"You don't have to be in Belhaven. You can come—"

"To your house? You know that's bullshit. Your husband made it pretty clear how he feels about me."

To my incredible shame, I could not argue with that. But if she was in Belhaven, it was only because I would be paying for it. And paying for it only happened because of the senator. She knew that and punished me anyway. I knew it would be this way when I accepted the proposal. Oddly, that didn't make it any better.

"You used to tell me what you were thinking," she said. "I don't know what you're thinking."

"That I'm glad you're safe."

"I'm fine. I'm safe. I . . ." I could hear her take a deep breath. "I went after that fucking asshole who raped the twelve-year-old."

Of course she did. This was how her psychosis worked. She was judge, jury, and executioner in her mind. "Did you . . . hurt him?"

"No. I didn't even get close to him."

But she would have hurt him. This was my nightmare four years ago, all over again.

You can't do this, I thought. *You can't do this to me again. I can't do this again. There is no other part of my life I have left to give up to save you.*

"What stopped you?" I asked.

"Not what . . . who. That fucking guy you hired to watch me."

"I didn't hire anyone."

"Then your prison guard husband did."

I took a deep breath, because I didn't know that, and it was entirely within the realm of possibility that the senator would do that. And not tell me. "You know that what you do . . . it reflects on him."

"Yeah. I fucking know that. And frankly the best thing for that asshole is if he'd just keel over and die."

The ceiling in the front sitting room had a

mural on it. A sky at dawn kind of thing. A warm glow around the edges. The lights hung in the middle of clouds. It was ridiculous. I paid a lot of money for it.

This was the part I could never say out loud but part of last week, part of not knowing where she was, was hoping she might be *here*. Hoping the evil person she was stalking was the senator.

Which was worse, I wondered, *the weapon or the person who wanted to use the weapon?*

"I'm sorry, Poppy," my sister said.

"I know." I took a deep breath and let it out slow.

"No really, I am. I know . . ."

"Just stop doing this." This vigilante revenge thing my sister could not stop herself from on her own. If left to her own devices and brain chemistry, she would right the wrongs perpetrated on young girls all over the world. And there was a lot about it that was admirable, but she did it with a knife. With violence. She wanted justice in blood.

"You know it's not that simple."

Yeah. I knew it. I'd been living with my sister's psychosis since she was sixteen and I was eighteen. Managing it. Cleaning up after it. Trying to find ways to funnel it into something useful.

Zilla was a genius, and by rights she should be able to do anything she set her formidable mind to. When it was healthy. She tried law school, thinking that might help her find the justice she craved. But the stress sent her into a manic phase that nearly killed her. I urged her to apply to the police academy and when she didn't pass the psych eval, social work. But when she left in the middle of her second week of school, I settled for keeping her safe.

And contained.

Belhaven.

The last two years she'd been in and out of care between Belhaven and her apartment I paid for in Brooklyn.

"Remember that pond at the back of the property in Bishop's Landing?" Zilla asked.

"Of course." That pond had been magic in a childhood without a lot of magic. The willow tree beside it had been a fort and a secret play place and safe. Safe most of all. More home than our actual house.

"Dad wanted to drain it. Said it was a breeding ground for mosquitos and that we would wander down there and drown."

"Yeah," I sighed. "So Mom taught us how to swim in it."

"He was so mad."

"But she won the fight, right?"

"Yep. And she won the fight with all the staff that tried to keep us away from it, too," I said. The housekeepers and tutors, even Monsieur Belleville the chef who tried to tempt us away from frog-catching with cakes and cookies.

"I'm fighting for the pond right now," my sister whispered.

"What's the pond in this scenario?" I asked.

"You. Us. The willow tree. The frogs. The way things used to be."

I let out my breath as slow as I could, curbing the rising tide of tears. "I know," I said. "I know."

"Don't be mad at me," Zilla whispered.

"Me? Mad at you? I can never be mad at you."

"Well, that's a lie."

"Fine," I said with a laugh because that was what she wanted. "I can never *stay* mad at you."

"You can come see me in two weeks," Zilla said. I was silent. Because the senator wouldn't allow it. Not without some wild story and help from the staff, who would eventually turn on me, resulting in some painful punishment.

The last time he'd taken my phone away and didn't let me leave the house for a month. I'd been bored, yes. Lonely. Terrified. But the real repercussion of it all was that all those people who called and texted me, who offered lunch dates and tickets to galas, who asked if I wanted to be on boards or fundraising committees—they all vanished. And when the month was over I was even more alone than I'd been before.

As punishment it had been wildly effective.

"Please come visit me, Pops. Pops—" her voice broke, and so did I. My nickname in my sister's voice was one of my favorite sounds in the world, and I was so scared for my sister and by my sister.

But she was all I had left, and I loved her so much. And it would be worth the punishment. It always was.

"Of course," I said. "I love you, Zilla."

The phone clicked twice, which was the end of the amount of allotted time I had to talk to my sister who was locked up in what was an insane asylum with a fancy name.

I listened to the echoing silence for a few seconds before hanging up, sitting limp in the chair. Relief and guilt and anger tossing bombs at each other in my stomach. And my heart.

My love for my sister was so complicated. And I wished that it could be easier. And then felt guilty for that wish.

A deep breath and the last of the adrenaline rippled out of my system and I sat, wrung-out in the chair I'd collapsed in.

God, it was an uncomfortable chair. It was uncomfortable, and I'd picked it out. I'd picked it out and had it reupholstered to match the couch and the area rug. All varying shades of blue and grey. Bits of pink and turquoise to match the vases on the coffee table. I'd just finished this room. Because I'd spent a year on the kitchen. And another two months on all the bathrooms. In another three months I would have redone this whole house.

I was good at it. That was a surprise. I liked it. A little. Enough to let it fill my days, to soothe the relative frustration at somehow not being able to do what I really wanted. I thought if I put enough of myself into this house it would start to feel like a home.

But I knew the truth: I was just redecorating my very gilded cage.

The front doorbell rang, and the sound was so surprising I started like I'd done something wrong. The senator was in his study on the other side of the house, so it wasn't him coming home. There wasn't an event, so it couldn't be hair and makeup. And no one ever *visited* me.

Anne the housekeeper came down the hallway, glancing at me, and we shared a quick look of surprise. Which was frankly more than we'd shared in the six months she'd been working here.

Look at us, bonding.

I kept myself in the chair, trying not to get my hopes up. Because I would love to have someone visit. To take my mind off Zilla, to alleviate just a little of my crushing boredom.

But it was probably some guy selling vacuums. *People still do that, don't they?*

Though probably not in Bishop's Landing.

I heard a familiar voice and jumped up out of my chair, rushing out into the hallway to see Caroline Constantine standing in the open doorway. She wore cream. Cream pants, heels, a blush shell, and a cashmere wrap. The trees were all changing colors, and she was lit up by a bright red maple behind her in my front yard. She was so beautiful she took my breath away.

Anne walked past me back towards the kitchen, leaving me alone with Caroline.

"Caroline?" It was shocking. A delight. And also so strange it felt like a dream. "Did I miss a lunch date?"

"You didn't miss anything, darling," Caroline said and then wrapped me in her arms, and I don't want to sound melodramatic, but I just folded right into that hug. I just collapsed into it. Caroline smelled like lavender body powder and Chanel No 5. She'd been my mother's best friend growing up, and hugging her felt like getting hugged by my mother.

"Then what are you doing here?" I asked, suddenly aware of what I looked like. I didn't wear makeup unless I was leaving the house, and my blonde hair was going red at the roots because I'd cancelled the last trip to the salon. I was in yoga pants and a long-sleeved sweatshirt that was damp down the back from trying to build a shower outside by the pool.

My latest project.

"I was supposed to be meeting Jim, but I realized one of my employees could handle it so I thought I would visit you instead," Caroline said. "Unless you're busy?"

"No. Not at all." I laughed. "Have a seat, and Anna can get us some tea."

Caroline, whose hair was that perfect three-step process blonde/silver/grey that made her look young and chic and somehow like she just rolled out of bed and off the beach at the same time, shook her head. "Darling, let's just go to the kitchen and have tea there. Don't bother Anna."

I remembered all those afternoons at Caroline's after Mom died when Zilla was just starting to fall apart. Barrels of strong tea with sugar and milk as she helped me figure out my life. As she saved me, really.

"Absolutely," I said, and I tucked my arm in hers, about to lead her to the kitchen when I realized there was a man still standing in the doorway. A dark suit against that blood-red tree. It took a second for him to register but when he did, I couldn't swallow my gasp.

The stranger. From my engagement party.

Right there in my doorway. His face had healed, and he looked . . . breathtaking.

I was suddenly lightheaded.

"Hi!" I said so inanely.

"This is Ronan," Caroline said, gesturing back to Ronan who was still in the doorway.

I opened my mouth to say we met, but Ronan was looking at me blankly, like he'd never seen me before.

"Nice to meet you," I said, shoving down my inappropriate delight.

"And you," he said. His accent rolled down my hallway and right through my body.

"I can show you where my husband's office is," I volunteered thinking of the few minutes it would take to walk down that wood-paneled hallway to his office.

"Don't be silly, Poppy," Caroline said. "Let Anna do it."

"Of course," I said. It was outrageous to be jealous of my housekeeper.

But I was.

Outside of our driver, Theo, Ronan was literally the last man I was ever alone with. All of my doctors' appointments, Jim was right there at my side. The doting husband, making sure our stories matched up.

The senator had been having meetings in his office at home more and more lately. Guests usually came in through the side entrance. His secretary signing people in and out.

It was nice that Caroline came through the front door to say hello.

"Follow me," Anna said to Ronan, having arrived as if summoned. Anna spent a lot of time waiting just around corners, always within earshot. Jim had said it was the sign of an excellent servant. I thought perhaps it was the sign of an excellent spy.

Of course, I did not say that out loud.

Ronan walked past us in the hallway, and I did not imagine the smell of smoke that wafted off him, and without thinking about it, I practically pasted myself to the wainscoting so there was no chance that his body might touch mine. Things were very precarious in my life, and I had the stupid sense that if he touched me, accidentally brushed his hand across mine, parts of my life would just crumble.

At the doorway, he turned and looked at us over his shoulder. I expected a smile. That man I met at my engagement party, he'd been the type to look over his shoulder and smile at a girl.

But there was no smile, and beside me Caroline gave him a sharp nod and he left.

Maybe he didn't remember me. That was possible. I was forgettable. My husband had forgotten me plenty over the last two years. I'd forgotten myself.

There was no reason that it should hurt that the stranger had forgotten me.

Ronan.

"Come, darling," Caroline said, putting her arm through mine. "Show me this big kitchen reno you've been working on."

I led my old friend through the hallway to the back of the house where the kitchen looked out over the pool and the pool house that I'd converted to a gym and yoga studio that I didn't use. But wanted to. The kitchen was filled with bright light and trying to look at it critically through Caroline's eyes, it was still a beautiful room. Marble countertops and gold fixtures. Built in dishwashers and two ovens. Beautiful old chandeliers over the long island with the gold stools. It was pretty. It felt like a room a person would want to spend time in. A room that could make a home. So, why didn't it? I wondered. Why didn't it feel like my home?

That thought crept into my head far too often. Filled me with a kind of panic that didn't do me any good. Feeling nothing was the only thing that made my life bearable.

I put the kettle on and pulled out the tea service Caroline had given me as a wedding gift.

"The house looks amazing, darling," she said, taking off her wrap and putting it over the edge of the island and pulling up a stool. She was a beautiful woman. Ageless and elegant. Inspiring really. The head of the Constantine family and the Chairwoman of the Board.

An absolute queen.

"Thank you. It's been a labor of love."

"How is Jim?" she asked.

Different, I wanted to say. He doesn't sleep. Rarely eats with me anymore. His temper—

always mercurial—was completely unpredictable. The other night after waking up alone just after midnight, I actually went looking for him. Not something I ever did before. Only to find him talking to himself in the kitchen. Muttering and swearing. I left without saying a word, but lay in bed staring at the ceiling, a sick dread in my stomach.

"Fine," I said, because I didn't know how to talk about Jim. Not with Caroline, not with anyone.

"How are things at the foundation?"

I took a deep breath. "On hold for the moment." My job at the foundation had been a sham, though it took me a while to realize it. I'd thought, stupidly, Jim was giving me a chance to actually do some good. But he'd taken it away as quickly as he'd given it to me.

Embarrassed, I hadn't told Caroline that. I'd lied, pretending I still worked there.

Pride and all.

"Really?" she asked. "You had such plans."

"After the miscarriage, we thought it best if I did less."

"Of course," Caroline said quickly. She didn't like talking about my miscarriages. And she had made it clear that she was not a shoulder for me to lean on when it came to my marriage. The first time I'd gone to her house, crying and bloody, in shock from Jim's violence, Caroline cleaned me up and told me it was my job to make it work. That I needed to make it work. For my own sake. For Zilla's sake.

And she sent me back to Jim.

Zilla would have told her to fuck off and taken a match to Jim's house. But, again, I was not Zilla, and I had dried my eyes and did what Caroline told me.

Somehow, making it work, meant me becoming smaller and smaller inside my body and life. I was unnoticeable and forgettable and passive and meek, all so I could survive. So my sister could survive.

"And Zilla? How is she?" Caroline asked.

"Belhaven."

"She checked herself back in?"

I nodded and didn't tell her about the seven days my sister had been gone. Caroline had already done so much for us, and there was nothing she could do that would change Zilla's circumstances.

And maybe I was embarrassed. Or maybe I was just exhausted.

"Good."

I lied and she smiled like all was well, and that too was a comfort. Pretending everything was fine was simply a way of making things fine.

I poured the boiling water into the teapot and tossed in three scoops of my special English Breakfast blend, got out some milk for the small milk pitcher, and sugar cubes. "Lemon?"

"No, thank you. Sit down." She pulled me down onto the stool next to her.

"You're very thin," she said, eyeing me up and down.

"The miscarriage—"

"Was months ago. Have you seen your doctor?"

"Of course."

"And you're okay?"

"Who is that man?" I asked. Blurted, really. "Ronan?"

"Are you changing the subject?" Caroline asked with a smile.

"I am," I said. "I don't want to talk about the miscarriage."

"Well, he's a man I hired a few years ago. He works on sensitive issues for the family."

"Why is he talking to Jim?"

"Just clarifying his position on the trade deal with China before the Senate vote."

"But what—"

"Darling," she said and began to pour us tea, "this conversation is why I hired Ronan. So I wouldn't have to have it."

"Of course," I said.

Caroline's smile was very pretty. I mean, she was a beautiful woman, who paid a lot of money to look twenty years younger than she was. I had seen her smile with her teeth and the recipients of those smiles shirked away, wondering what they'd done wrong.

But the smiles she gave me always seemed different. Softer. Kinder.

"I have something for you." She reached into her purse and pulled out an envelope. When Dad first died there'd been lots of these envelopes filled with cash to help with Zilla, to get me an apartment after the banks took what was left of the house. To buy me clothes when the bank took my clothes. But when it was clear what Dad had really done, the envelopes stopped, and Jim was mentioned.

"I don't need that," I said. Though I thought a little of the envelope of my own in my underwear drawer where I'd been squirreling away cash. Not a lot. I didn't get a lot of cash in my life. But some of the trades wanted cash, and I told Jim they asked for a couple hundred dollars more, and I pocketed the rest.

Every time I put money in that envelope my mind was blank. Like I had no real idea what I was doing or why I was doing it. But at night, when I couldn't sleep, I sometimes counted the money and wondered how much I needed to get free when Jim went too far.

And then I wondered what was too far?

Certainly, the night of the miscarriage . . . that had been too far. And yet, I was still here.

"Look inside," Caroline said, smiling. "You're going to be happy."

I slid the envelope across the granite and opened it up, only to find old photographs.

"Oh my," I gasped. Tears sharp and hot and sudden in my eyes. "It's Mom."

"Her sixteenth birthday and then," she reached forward and pulled out one from the back, "a random Halloween and our high school graduation."

"Look at you," I sighed. They were both so beautiful and young. Mom wore a lace mini-dress at her birthday with long belled sleeves. Her long hair was parted down the middle, and her eyeliner was thick and black. Beside her, Caroline was wearing a black and white sequined mini dress with white boots. The 1970's in full glorious effect.

"I'd give my leg for that dress back. And those legs," Caroline said. "That night your mother stole a bottle of champagne and snuck on the roof and took off her dress. She drank that champagne in her underwear on the roof, and I thought her father was going to kill her."

"He sent her away," I said. "After that, didn't he?"

"Boarding school in Connecticut. She stole a car at Thanksgiving and came down and snuck in my room." Caroline's smile was nearly heartbreaking with its tenderness. "She was . . ."

Troubled. A problem. Reckless. All those words could have applied. And I'd heard them plenty over the years. But all of that recklessness and danger had another side. And I knew all this all too well after the years with my sister. The light that came off my sister was worth some of the darkness. My mom was the same way, and only Caroline, my sister, and I understood the beauty of that kind of light.

It was part of why I forgave her for sending me back to Jim that night. It was part of why I always welcomed her into my home with open arms. We'd been through fire together.

"Amazing," I said. Looking down at my gorgeous young mother burning far too bright.

"She really was."

There was the click of the door shutting down the hallway, and suddenly Ronan was in my kitchen. Tall and thin, tugging the sleeves of his shirt down beneath the cuff of his jacket.

"You're done then?" Caroline said.

"I am," he said, and then he glanced at me, and I was frozen in his cold blue gaze.

"Would you like some tea?" I asked, remembering how I'd thought that night that I could sense warmth in him. There was no part of this man that was warm. He was ice, through and through.

What happened to that charming man in the shadows who'd made me laugh? He'd also pressed my lip into my teeth until I bled, but honestly, I'd pushed that memory away. That thought. Unable to hold it in my head with the same memories of the way the senator hurt me. Both made me bleed.

Why was one somehow exciting to me? The other abhorrent? I didn't know how to hold both things in my hands at once.

Though, he was probably wondering the same kind of thing about me. That shy girl, cracking jokes and drinking out of a flask. That girl with her red hair and her ridiculousness, she was nowhere to be found.

Two years had happened. Two very long years, perhaps for both of us.

"We have to go," Caroline said, her voice cooler than it had been with me, which was how Caroline talked to all her employees. Nothing personal. Ever.

Caroline kissed my cheek. "Don't bother seeing us out. I know the way."

She left me in a cloud of her perfume, and Ronan stepped out of her way, letting Caroline breeze by him, and in her absence, our eyes met again.

And I smiled, I smiled like we were old friends. Like we shared a secret. Like I . . . I don't know, it was weird. It was stupid, but I smiled at him like I missed him. Because he'd been the last person I'd talked to who had no idea who I was. Or who I was married to. He was the last person who'd offered me whiskey and a piece of cheese and to beat someone up for me—just because.

No one had been as kind to me for two years.

And I always got stupid around kindness.

But he didn't seem to recognize me.

I was standing close to him. Closer than I'd

been to any man who wasn't the senator. Close
enough to see his eyelashes. His pulse in his
throat. And his eyes went to my throat, and I
wondered if maybe he was looking at *my* pulse. If
he was thinking of my heartbeat and that was a
ridiculous thing to think.

"You changed your hair," he said, surprising
me. And like I was a debutante in a movie, I
touched the blonde curl hanging over my
shoulder.

"I did." Nice. Excellent conversational skills.
"Your face healed up."

"It always does."

That made me smile, that small glimmer of
the man from the party. Making light of dark
things. I wished I could be that way, instead of
this petrified rabbit I'd become.

"What happened to your neck?" he asked, and
I realized my sweatshirt had gotten pulled aside
enough to reveal the bruise on my collarbone.

"It's not what you think," I said.

"It's not a bruise?"

"I fell." I winced at how terrible that sounded.
I put my hand over the bruise where I could feel
it, hot and ugly under my skin. The senator had
thrown a book at me. It did not escape me that
he'd thrown it at my head, and I'd flinched so

he'd missed.

And that's not too far?

"Sure you did," he said. "Did it hurt?"

I was about to say no, but then I realized what he was asking. What question was buried deep beneath that one. Not 'did it hurt'? But 'was I surviving'? Because if it still hurt, if I gave the senator that power over my body, then I would never make it. Maybe I was wrong, maybe that wasn't what he was asking. But it's what I heard, and that was all that mattered.

And I wished, god, how I wished I could lie, I lied to everyone else in my life about the senator. But somehow—with this stranger—the lie didn't come. And instead, the truth slipped out.

"Yes," I said. "It hurt."

His lips pressed tight, and he nodded as if the information was just so disappointing to him, but what could you do? And I wanted to ask him how I could make it not hurt. Like what magic was required.

But he turned and left without another word. He left me alone with my empty house and my bruises.

Three months later, my husband committed suicide in his office. Shot himself in the head. A doctor's record that he had advanced brain cancer splattered in blood on the desk in front of him.

CHAPTER FOUR

LEONARD BARRINGTON, ESQ., was written in gold on the glass door in front of me. The Q was flaking off. I wonder if the senator knew about that Q. He did not like imperfections. The urge to scrape it all off with my thumbnail was powerful. But I curled my hands into fists and resisted.

"We don't have to do this," Zilla said over my shoulder.

We stood at the door of the lawyer's office in Bishop's Landing. A cottage building down the hill from the house. I just needed to push the door open. And walk in. There was a cold drizzly rain falling down on us, dripping from my hair onto the bare skin of my neck. The cold of it was an icy pain.

"I've put it off twice," I whispered, the words caught in my throat. The senator's lawyer had been patient and understanding but putting it off one more time would be ridiculous. The funeral was two months ago, and I was running out of excuses to not meet with him. But still I wasn't pushing open that door.

"You want to go get a drink? We don't have—"

"I'm scared," I said.

"I know." Zilla put her arm around my waist, holding me up. She'd been here with me since the senator died, doing exactly this. Holding me up. "But it won't be like when Dad died."

My breath caught, and I let it out as slow as I could. "It will be worse." How could it not? The one constant in my life was the senator wanted to hurt me. His being dead seemed unlikely to change that. When Dad died there was no money, and I survived. But leaving me with no money seemed the least of what the senator might do to me.

"It doesn't matter," Zilla said. "We'll be fine. We will be absolutely fine. You can move in with me in New York. You can go back to school—"

"Stop," I breathed. No dreaming. No planning. It never worked out for me. "Let's just . . . get this over with."

I pushed open the door to the office, and Zilla ran interference with a secretary. Soon we had tea I wasn't going to drink and were sitting in leather chairs in front of a large desk across from Mr.

Bennington, the senator's lawyer who always reminded me of a Keebler elf. He wore a lot of sweater vests and glasses. Nice enough, but looks were deceiving. I never understood why the senator, with all his connections, had this man as a personal lawyer.

"I'm glad you could make it in," he said. "I have some paperwork for you to take home. The senator was doing some work on the foundation, and he had a trust for his future children, but we never finalized the paperwork. There is also the deed for the house." He gestured behind him to a box on the edge of the desk.

The future children bit kind of hit me right in the chest, and I sat there silent.

"We can take that," Zilla said and took the box off the desk and balanced it on her lap. She was clear these days. Present. The summer stay at Belhaven long behind her. She was doing what the doctors told her, and in the months since Jim shot himself, she'd been indispensable to me.

Not because she made me tea and helped me send thank you notes and boxed up the senator's clothes for donation, but because she went for long walks with me in the cold spring March mornings.

"Do you want to go back?" I'd ask her.

"Nope," she'd lie through pale lips.

She made dinner out of things I hadn't had in two years. Pizza delivered to our door. Macaroni and cheese. Veggies dipped in ranch dressing. Goldfish crackers. The food of that summer. Of our childhood.

Freedom.

Because in the middle of the night when I left the king-size bed I'd shared with Jim and crawled into the guest bed with her, she didn't say anything. She put her arm around me and curled up tight.

And she didn't ask me if I was all right. Everyone in the world was asking me if I was all right, but she knew that everything I was feeling was so much more complicated than just 'all right.'

I wasn't happy or sad. Or relieved. I was nauseous and scared. Jumpy. Unsure. A rabbit out of its cage. I was a mess, and she knew it. And didn't try to change it.

She just took care of me.

"The will is very straightforward," he said, adjusting his Keebler glasses on his nose. *He left it all to a charity,* I thought. *To his foundation. He left it to another woman. He left it to another woman, and he sold me to another man.*

God, I was really spiraling.

"As his only family and heir, you get everything," he said, flipping through a file. "The house. The cars. The bank accounts, equalling—" He turned another page. "5.2 million."

He looked at us over the top of his glasses. Zilla shook her head, and I found it hard to breathe. "Dollars?" Zilla finally asked.

"Yes," he said with a smile. "That's standard."

"What's the catch?" I asked.

"There . . . ah . . . is no catch," he said, glancing at Zilla and back at me.

"No." I stood, panicked and more scared than I was before. "There's a catch. There's always a catch." Every gift from him was a double-edged sword. Nothing was free. Nothing was safe.

"With the senator?" he asked.

"Does it say my name? Show me—"

"Poppy," Zilla said, reaching out to touch my arm. "Calm down."

"It's right here," he said. Standing up and holding out the paper. "He wrote his will just after you were engaged. He was very clear. His wife would get everything. Are you all right?"

"Perhaps if we could have a second," Zilla said.

"No. No. Let's just do this." I wanted to go home. The rabbit longing for her cage.

I signed paperwork where he pointed as the truth hovered somewhere above real comprehension in my brain. An hour later, we carried the box out with us. I could only sit in Zilla's car.

"Poppy?" Zilla said.

"Yeah?"

"You're rich. You're rich, and you're free."

"I am," I said, watching the rain hit the windshield and splatter.

"You still think there's a catch?" she asked.

"There always is."

"Maybe . . . the catch was everything before? Being married to him. Maybe—karmically—you've already paid for this. Maybe this is only good."

I actually laughed at her.

"Pops. You have everything he had. It's all yours now."

"Everything," I said.

"It hasn't sunk in?"

"Not even a little."

Zilla started the car. "It will. Just give it some time."

We pulled out of the small parking lot behind the lawyer's office and headed for the road up the hill to the mansions. My mansion. Zilla chatted away about dinner and maybe getting a bottle of champagne, and her words flowed over and through me. Until there was only one truth left. The one I'd been pushing away and pretending didn't exist.

"You need to go home. Back to the city," I blurted.

"What?" she said, looking at me and then back at the road. "What are you talking about?"

"You can't babysit me forever. I need to move on, and you need to go back to your life."

"I want to stay," Zilla said. "I should stay."

I wanted her to stay so badly I could taste it. The house was warmer when she was in it. I felt less like Jim's widow and more like . . . I don't know. Something between Jim's wife and that girl I'd been. But I wasn't either of those things anymore.

I was something else entirely. And it was time to figure out what that was.

And Zilla finally had her feet under her. I couldn't take that away because I was lonely.

"It is in fact insane that I would leave you," Zilla said. "And I know insane."

"That's not funny."

"It is. A little." She smiled at me, but I didn't take the bait.

"You have a life to get back to," I said.

"School?"

"Poppy," she sighed. "It's my first year of nursing school. I can defer a semester."

"No. You're not going to defer anything on my account. You're just getting back on track."

"You realize you're saying Fundamentals of Nursing is more important than the total unravelling of my sister's life, and I am here to tell you it is not." She grinned at me. The grin it was impossible not to return. God, Zilla could be so fun, and I couldn't remember the last time I had fun.

Ronan in the dark at the party, my brain supplied, as if it had been waiting for the chance to remind me.

"Come on, let me take care of you, Pops," she said. "You fired the senator's secretary. You fired the housekeeper. You're alone."

"I still have Theo."

"Yeah, and if you knew how to drive you'd get rid of him, too."

She wasn't wrong. I studied her profile.

Zilla was a stunner. Olive skin and dark hair cut short and edgy, making the most of her delicate features from my mother's side of the family. She had a tiny frame she covered in tight shirts, dark denim and high heeled boots. I was a giraffe compared to her. All elbows and hips. Long red hair I dyed blonde because . . . well, because the senator liked it that way.

My sister looked like a punk imp. And not at all like the type of person who'd held a knife to a priest's genitals after he'd been caught abusing young boys.

But it was hard to guess what that kind of person looked like.

No matter what Zilla looked like, she was a twenty-one-year-old woman in nursing school. A woman with a future she could finally see and grab a hold of, and I wanted no part of derailing that. I was a widow at 22. Full of dust and fear.

"I don't need taking care of," I lied. Or maybe it wasn't a lie. I didn't need taking care of. I wasn't injured or prostrate with grief, it was just nice. Nice to be someone else's priority for a second.

She parked in the long driveway, and we stepped out of the car. I grabbed the box from the lawyer from the back seat.

"We should go through that," Zilla said.

"Not today," I said. Maybe never.

"You want me to put it in the office?"

See? I should be stronger. I should be able to say, no, I can do it. But I wasn't that strong. Not yet. I nodded, and my sister took the box of paperwork to my husband's office. A room I hadn't been in since he died and, truthfully, if I had my way, I would never go into again.

I made tea and strengthened my case for Zilla to get back to her life.

We argued that night and for another week, but finally I won and Zilla packed her bags. The day she was leaving, she came into the kitchen with her roller bag, and I knew what she was going to say before she said it.

"Don't," I told her, thinking I might cut her off. But no one got in the way of Zilla and what she wanted to say.

"Hear me out. You said you wanted independence, and the only person you've kept is your driver. Let me teach you how to drive and you can fire him, too! You like firing people." Her eyebrows were cocked, the devil in her bright eyes. "We can cut your hair. Get drunk. Like really smashed. We haven't done that. Oh!" she said like she suddenly had a great idea. "Getting laid. How about that? A little rebound action with some random at a bar. I'll be your wingman. Doesn't that sound good?"

"No. Not at all."

"Okay, you can be my wingman."

"I would be a terrible wingman."

"It's true. But I'm willing to give you a try."

I laughed until it caught on a sob.

"I can stay," Zilla said, her voice soft. "I want to stay. My course load this semester is light, and I can take it all online, right here from your kitchen. Let me take care of you. We don't have to do anything." She stroked back my hair. "Except get your hair back to its natural color. This blonde is so Stepford wife I can't take it. Or! Let's leave. You're rich now. Let's go meet randoms in a bar in Tahiti?"

I pulled Zilla into a fierce hug, holding her so hard hoping maybe to absorb some of her fire, hoping maybe she would absorb some of my calm. "I'm all right. I am. I haven't been alone in years, Zilla. Let me just . . . be alone. Please," I said. "I will call you if that changes."

"It feels so bad to leave you, though."

"I know. I do. But, trust me, please, this is what I want."

"You promise?"

"I promise. But are you going to be okay?"

"Oh my god, you have hit peak, Poppy. Worrying about me? Now?"

"Habit."

"I'll be fine. I'll be worrying about you."

Theo, my driver, the only employee I had left, opened the front door. He'd taken Zilla's car to gas it up and top up the fluids. He didn't say anything or do anything. But I knew by the nearly inaudible scrape of his shoe on the tile. The sudden change in the air. The chill up my spine that said I wasn't alone.

When was that going to end?

Would it?

I swallowed back my sob and let my sister walk out the door.

And in the quiet she left behind, I immediately felt something like panic. Like . . .emotion. Like a scream I couldn't scream. I grabbed the tools I used to help work on the house, and I went to the pool deck and finally finished the shower by the pool.

It took so much less time than I thought it would. Too little time, really. I needed it to take hours. A month. But within forty-five minutes I pulled the chain and water poured out of the rain showerhead I'd picked out months ago.

I let go of the chain, and it stopped. The water disappearing down the black drain.

It worked. I built a shower.

This was another skill I could add to the application for the catering company.

Experience: eating canapes, mitigating the physical pain my husband wanted to inflict on me, and making outdoor showers.

"Who wouldn't hire me?" I joked out loud. If Zilla was here, she would laugh. But she wasn't, so I just sounded like a crazy woman.

I pulled the chain again, and water came pouring out, splashing over my flipflops and the legs of my pants. I did it. I could still do things. I had enough small power inside of me to make something happen. Even this little thing.

He had not taken everything away from me.

Oh, he'd taken plenty. Some things he'd taken in great handfuls. Giant pieces. My dreams of being a teacher. My education. My autonomy. And some I'd simply handed him, learning quickly that my dignity meant more to him than it did to me. And now I owned this house. Everything that had been his. Everything he'd taken from me, I had a chance to get back.

How? How does someone do that? Like, in what drawer would I find my ambition? My confidence? Was my faith on a bookshelf in his office? I imagined finding those things, putting them on like jewelry. Too-big rings that would fall off my fingers.

Who the fuck am I anymore?

Fully dressed, I stepped into the shower, letting the warm water pour over me until something in me thawed. The ice I'd formed around myself melted.

And then I sobbed bitter angry tears. My husband had been sick and scared and in pain, and he'd killed himself with a gun I didn't know he had.

Then I cried more, because he'd turned me into someone I didn't recognize.

Because I was just so relieved he was gone.

And happy. I was so happy I laughed through my tears. I was howling with laughter and sobs. A total mess.

This was why I needed my sister to go live her life. Because I needed to lose my mind a little.

The hot water ran out, and the early spring night was freezing.

Dripping wet and steaming into the cooler air, I stepped out of the shower across the pool deck through the sliding glass doors into the kitchen. This—dripping puddles across the floor would have enraged the senator. I couldn't remember the last time I'd made a decision born of my own desires rather than just reacting to him. Reacting to fear.

My phone on the edge of the counter, which

had gone completely dark a week after the funeral, was bright again with an incoming message.

From Caroline.

Come to my office tomorrow in the city. We have much to discuss.

Thank god, I thought, and braced myself against the counter.

Something to do.

CHAPTER FIVE

THE NEXT MORNING, I got dressed and put on makeup and my sharp black suit with the grey silk shell, and I sat in the backseat of my husband's town car that I now owned as I was driven into New York City to see Caroline.

And I was excited. Excited by the drive from the rolling green lawns and the mansions of Bishop's Landing down the interstate into Manhattan. Excited to *do* something.

It started to rain, and the umbrellas sprouted on street corners, and the air got that smell of wet cement. We stopped at a red light, and kids were streaming out of a school, jumping over puddles.

Even through the glass of the window I could hear them laughing.

I should get a hot dog. From one of those carts. I hadn't had one of those in years. And perhaps after the meeting a short stroll through Central Park. *No, it was raining, and the senator would want me back . . .*

The senator was dead, and I could do whatever the hell I wanted.

What did I want? Lord, the thought was paralyzing. I could feel my heart start to pound in my neck. The reality of my freedom making me short of breath. Sweat bloomed along my hairline. Two years with him. Three months with his memory, and I had no idea who I was anymore.

Stop. Breathe.

I didn't have to experience all my freedom all at once. I wanted a hot dog. I could start there.

The Constantines owned a giant high-rise office building in Manhattan where Winston ran Halcyon. But Caroline owned a brownstone on the Upper East Side across from the park. And that was where I'd been summoned.

The car pulled up to the curb, and Theo got out in the rain, popped open the umbrella and opened my door.

The memory came out with the cool fresh air. Like a missile hiding underwater.

"Stop," Jim said, grabbing my wrist. "Wait."

"I don't need someone to open the door for me," I said, pulling away, but his grip was unbreakable, and he got that look on his face that he was getting more and more. That half smile. That blank stare. I stopped fighting him, and he squeezed my wrist

harder.

"You're hurting me," I whispered.

"Am I?" he asked, suddenly and completely un-familiar to me. His handsome face was simply a mask over the reality of him. The awful snakey-ness of him.

"Jim—" I breathed.

"You wait for the driver to open the door," he said like I was a child. Like he needed to teach me. He dropped my wrist just as the driver opened the door. His face his own again. His smile the lie everyone believed.

"Ma'am?" Theo stood outside the door, his head framed by the umbrella behind him.

"Yes," I said, fighting the urge to rub away the phantom pain in my wrist. "Just a second."

Theo stood back. He was just a man. An employee. But he was also a reminder of what I'd been. A possession. If I wanted real independence, I did need to learn how to drive.

Perhaps this was too soon? Coming into the city? I hadn't been back here without Jim or without trying to hide what he did to me for over two years. But if I gave into this fear and went home, I knew there would never be a day when I was brave enough. It was now or never.

I had to get out of the car. I did. Caroline was

expecting me, and I loved Caroline, and I wanted a hot dog, and so I forced myself to get out of the car and stand in the drizzly rain. Theo didn't smile at me. He didn't seem like the smiling type, but I could tell he was proud of me.

I was proud of me. This was clearly a baby-steps situation.

"Mrs. Maywell," a serious man with a smart suit stood up from behind his desk when I walked in. "It's good to see you."

"You too." The banalities came so easy.

"We're all so sorry for your loss."

"Thank you," I said.

"Mrs. Constantine is waiting for you in her office," he said and led me to the elevator. I was embarrassed by this attention. By his kindness. I wanted him to sit down and ignore me. He pushed the button for the carriage. "Justin will meet you by the elevators."

I smiled and thanked him. The elevator whisked me to the eighth floor and Justin, Caroline's assistant, greeted me at the door. It was like I couldn't be alone, even for a minute. Was that standard, I wondered? Or was everyone just so convinced I was helpless.

"Hello, Mrs. Maywell—"

"Poppy," I all but snapped. I couldn't stand

that name. It made me feel owned. I smiled. "Please, call me Poppy."

"Of course. Caroline will be two minutes. Can I get you some coffee?"

"No. I'm fine."

Justin led me across the waiting room to Caroline's office. The rugs were burgundy Turkish silk. There were leather couches and chairs for people to wait in. He led me right past them to the double wooden doors with beautiful lion's head doorknobs in the middle of them. There was another door leading off from this room. An office for one of her children, I imagined. Which one of them had the honor of sharing space with her I didn't know.

"Mrs. Constantine said you should wait in here," Justin said and opened the door to Caroline's inner sanctum.

I sat and waited to see what was in store for me now. Waiting, always waiting to see what was going to happen to me next.

"Did anyone offer you a drink?" Caroline said as she swept in.

I jumped. "Everyone," I said. "You have very thorough staff."

"Well, don't let them know that or I might have to give them a raise. Now," Caroline sat down on her side of the desk and shot me a level look. "How are you doing?"

"Good!" I said, too brightly. "Fine. I'm fine."

"Zilla headed home?"

How did she know that?

"Yesterday. And, before you ask, I'm fine with it."

Caroline gave me a long look that seemed doubtful. And I felt a strange and sudden spark of anger. I'd been watched for months now. Years. I didn't like it. Never liked it.

"You summoned me," I said. "Why am I here, Caroline?"

Caroline blinked at my tone and then flipped open a file.

"We're doing a charity fundraiser in two weeks, and we're going to give a posthumous award to the senator," Caroline said.

"All right," I said. Those sorts of things happened all the time. In Jim's office were stacks of framed letters and plaques from different charities honoring him as some kind of hero. "What do you need me for?"

"We need you there so we can present you with the award."

I started to shake my head. No. Nope. I didn't need to do that anymore. Jim was gone. My life as the smiling clapping wife in Vera Wang was over. I wasn't sure what was going to happen next, but it wasn't going to be that anymore.

"It's been months," Caroline said.

"What does that have to do with anything?"

"You are the face of his legacy. He had business ventures and legal obligations, and they're yours now."

"No." I shook my head again. "They're not. I'm his widow. That's all."

She tilted her head, and I sighed, sensing what was coming. "What do you want, Poppy?"

A hot dog. I just want a hot dog.

"Not . . . business ventures and legal obligations," I said. I didn't want to be the face of his legacy. I wanted a million miles between myself and him. I was going to change my name back to my maiden name. Dye my hair.

"What about the foundation?" She lifted her eyebrows, and I felt a tug. Old dreams that had been squished and pushed aside and forgotten. But I had no idea if I wanted those dreams anymore. I'd been so young. Twenty years old, fresh-faced and convinced I could help. Fresh-faced and hopeful.

God, I'd been so hopeful. The kind of hopeful that was just hollow now.

"There will be press at the fundraiser. It will be good for our company and good for the senator's foundation . . . which, I will remind you, is yours now. And you can do what you want with it. But the fundraiser will give you options. And I would think . . . options might appeal to you."

I stiffened, unable to look at her, but terribly aware of her looking at me. Was she saying the thing we never said? That I want options now because the senator stripped me of them?

Was she pitying me? Manipulating me?

Was I being distrustful because that was all I knew how to be now?

I shook off the thoughts and smiled.

"Okay," I said.

"Okay?" my dear friend and mentor lit right up. "I knew I could count on you."

I sat up straighter, trying to manage the strange nausea in my stomach.

"I'll have Justin send over the details. Do you want him to write a few remarks for you?"

"About the senator?" I asked. What in the world would I say about him?

Once, he broke my finger at the dinner table. One minute I was handing him a plate, the next he'd snapped my pinky finger back until it popped.

"That would be great," I said and stood up.

"Have Justin send me everything I need."

"You're not going to stay for lunch?"

"No, actually. I've got another engagement for lunch."

"With who?" Caroline asked. She asked like she was surprised. Like it was impossible I had friends. And she wasn't wrong, but I was allowed to have some dignity.

"Just a friend from college," I lied and picked up my purse. "I'll look forward to Justin's notes."

I left her office, aware of her concern chasing me out the door. Justin sat at his desk in her outer sanctum, and I gave him my breeziest smile. "I look forward to seeing you at the fundraiser!"

"Let me—" he said, standing up from his desk.

"I'm good. Take care." I pushed the button, and the elevator opened as if it had been waiting for me. Which, since it was Caroline's private elevator, it probably had been.

I heard one of the other doors open as I stepped inside, leaning back against the glass and marble. The low murmur of voices as the doors began to slide shut.

"She's leaving?" asked a brogue that made me stand up straight. *Was that . . .?*

Before the door could shut, a hand braced it open, and I came face to face with Ronan.

CHAPTER SIX

SPEECHLESS, I GAPED at him as he stepped into the elevator. The doors closed behind him, shrinking the square footage around us to absolutely nothing. I stepped back into the furthest corner of the elevator.

"What are you doing?" I asked. It was ingrained, being frantic alone with a man that wasn't Jim.

"Are you all right?" he asked, reaching for my elbow. And I absolutely flailed away from him so he wouldn't touch me.

"I'm fine," I said, embarrassed down to my core.

"You're a terrible liar." He dropped his hand without actually touching me, and I'd never been so relieved and disappointed in my life.

I laughed, low in my throat because he had no idea what a liar I could be.

He reached behind his back and pressed the button that stopped the elevator. We lurched to a halt, and I braced myself against the wall behind me so I wouldn't bounce into him.

"What are you doing?" I cried.

"Why are you upset?"

"Because you are like . . . kidnapping me?"

"Kidnapping?" His grin was . . . well, it was something. And I didn't like it. I didn't like how it made me feel. "Are you all right, Poppy?"

"Stop pretending you care!"

"Someone should care," he said, quietly. "Someone should care about you, Princess."

Oh god. Oh *god*.

"And you think you're the man to do that?" Why did I say that? He was making a mess of me with his concern and proximity. I was unused to both. "Never mind. I don't care."

"Do you want me to?"

"Of course not."

"Such a liar today. It's hard to believe you're the same girl I met at that party."

"Because I'm not," I snapped. He leaned a shoulder against the wall. Like we were two people chatting at a bar. A party. Any two people.

"Why are you upset, Poppy?"

I stared at his shirt. The white dress shirt, sleeves rolled up. The neck loose like he'd been working hard at something, but I couldn't imagine what this man worked hard at. "My husband died," I said, because I hadn't figured out why I was really upset.

"That's why you're near tears, running from Caroline's office?"

"Of course."

His grin was a direct shot to my chest. "What am I supposed to do with a girl with so many lies in her mouth?"

There was something . . . maybe the way he said *mouth*. Or the way he was looking at me. The tiny elevator. Any of it. All of it. But I got this sense, this very real sense that what he wanted to do to me was dirty.

And I could count the number of times I'd thought of something dirty in the last two years on one hand.

But at this moment, locked in an elevator with Ronan whose last name I didn't know, I imagined, in one white-hot second, him pushing me up against the wall. Stepping up tight against me. That lethal body of his pressed to mine.

A blush incinerated my face. My neck.

"Oh, what are you thinking?" he asked. His voice low. His smile a charming twist. "What dark thing am I doing to you in your mind?"

I swallowed, and he grinned like he was relishing my discomfort, and I realized that I was a toy to him, the same way I'd been a toy to my husband. It was just a different game.

"Make the elevator go," I said. The blush on my neck was gone, though that thought I'd had would haunt me.

"Tell me what you were thinking."

"That you only want to hurt me, like everyone else."

Something in him shifted; some unseen darkness leapt in his eyes. His face. But his expression didn't change.

I gave him no time for more sarcasm or false concern. Some half-baked flirtation for the pitiful widow. I reached past him, ignoring the warmth of his body and the smell of his skin and pressed the button that made the elevator resume its descent. Within seconds the door was open, and I walked around him towards freedom. Part of me expected him to follow. My husband was always going to have the last word. There was no situation where I was allowed to walk away.

But then, I was oddly disappointed when Ronan didn't.

My driver, of course, was waiting for me, back door open, and I knew that Justin had called him and told him I was on my way down. I slipped into my seat, and the door slammed behind me. When I turned, before the car drove off, I saw Ronan standing there. On the sidewalk, Caroline's building behind him, the madness of Manhattan spinning around him like he was the untouched, unmoved center of everything.

Ronan.

He didn't wave or take the ten steps it would take to open my car door and pull me out, and I was both relieved and upset that he didn't. Feeling foolish followed, of course, it always did. But still he stood there, looking at me, studying me through the glass of the door. Through the span of the two years and two other times we'd seen each other.

My pulse hammered in my throat—and it wasn't fear. It wasn't anything but the normal violence of being alive. Very alive.

"Where to, ma'am?" Theo asked.

"The nearest hot dog cart," I said, and we pulled away from the curb.

CHAPTER SEVEN

THE VALENTINO BALLGOWN swirled in shades of light blue around my bodice and flowed out into the skirt in indigo and then cobalt and black down to the floor. It was dramatic and elegant. Swishy around my legs and forgiving around my waist.

Suitable for mourning.

Jim's mother's black pearls were in my ears and around my neck. My hair, freshly dyed for the event, was blonde again and pulled up on top of my head in a tight bun. I had the particular kind of headache that comes from having your hair pulled back too tight. But it distracted me from my nerves.

The Prince George Ballroom was decorated in Caroline's traditional cream and gold. The cream roses and pale pink hydrangeas. It was breathtaking the first time I'd seen it and now, years later, it was still breathtaking. The power of classic.

Though there could be an argument that it

was enough already with the white roses.

"Poppy!" It was Julie Dunbar coming out of the bathroom I was lingering beside.

"Julie. It's so good to see you." We kissed each other's cheeks with equal fakeness.

"You look marvelous, darling," she said. "Again, Dean and I are just so sorry for your loss."

"Thank you," I said. A waiter went by with flutes of champagne, and I snagged one. *A drinking game*, I thought. Anytime anyone said they were sorry for my loss, I had to take a drink.

Oh, I thought. This was an excellent coping mechanism.

"He was a great man," Julie said, taking her own glass.

"Was he?"

"Pardon?"

"He was," I said and smiled my serene smile. "If you'll excuse me." I breezed past her and on the way to the door, three more people told me how sorry they were for my loss, and at the door to the ballroom, I got a new champagne glass.

I made a wide circle around the room, clinging to the outside where the shadows had the best chance of hiding me. But still, I was down another champagne glass by the time I was halfway through the room.

Looking over everyone it struck me, not just because I was a little tipsy. But I was so bored. So terribly bored with the dresses and the conversation. It wasn't just people being sorry for my loss, it was the conversation about trade deals and Supreme Court nominees. It was the traffic out of the city and where to eat and drink the best whatever-was-popular-now.

Who cares? I wanted to ask them. Are we all so shallow that this was all that mattered in our lives? Wasn't there more than this?

I can build a shower! Can any of you assholes do that?

"Hello, Princess."

Like I'd summoned him out of my boredom, there was Ronan.

In a tuxedo and his fallen-angel face.

He isn't boring.

"Fancy meeting you here," I said, and his eyebrow kicked up.

"Are you drunk?"

"Let me check," I said with a sigh and pretended to think it over. "I do believe I am."

His blue eyes glimmered, but his mouth set in a frown. My Irishman didn't approve.

"It's a drinking game," I explained. "Every time someone offers their *sincere* condolences, I have a drink. It's been effective."

"You shouldn't be drinking."

"Yeah, I considered that. Do you know," I said, "your eyes are smiling, but your face is not. How do you do that?" I attempted to copy his expression, but all I did was squint.

"You're going to be a problem for me," he said in a low tone. He gestured for a server, asking him for a cup of coffee and a plate of food.

"I'm not going to eat," I said.

"Of course not."

The coffee arrived, and he put in some sugar. A splash of cream.

"That's not how I drink my coffee," I said, like the joke was on him.

"It's not for you," he said and took a sip. He made a sound in his throat like it tasted good, and suddenly I wanted some coffee. But I was onto his reverse psychology.

"You work for Caroline," I said.

"I do." Another sip of coffee.

"What do you do for her?"

"Whatever she needs."

The last of my champagne went down easily, and suddenly at my elbow there was a cup of coffee.

"I'd like another glass of champagne," I told a

passing waiter, but beside me Ronan shook his head. A tiny imperceptible movement, but I was conditioned to see those little things. The danger, I'd learned the hard way was always in those little things.

"Fuck off, Ronan," I said under my breath and walked right past him. He caught my arm, touching me at the fragile bend of my elbow. His palm was big and wide where my skin was tender.

I gasped at the exquisite realness of it. The audacity of it.

"Poppy," he said, and I blinked, trying to pull out of his grasp. I was . . . raw where he touched me. I felt too much.

"I never told you my name," I said.

"You never had to."

"That night. Did you know who I was the whole time?" I whispered, asking a question that had sat in the back of my brain like a thorn. Unasked, but there. Steady and hurtful.

"Was I only nice to you because you were marrying the senator," he said. "Is that what you're asking?"

I said nothing, breathing hard through my nose, looking at the starched white collar of his shirt where it met the black silk of his lapel.

"No," he said quietly. "I didn't know who you

were until the senator came to the door."

His blue eyes caught me. Held me. And I couldn't pull against him. I could barely even breathe. It wasn't fear that held me. No. Not at all. It was something worse. Something I didn't have the slightest clue how to manage.

I felt the touch of his gaze on my face. My lips, and they parted so I could pull in a breath. My chest lifted, and he glanced down and away. His jaw tight, and I didn't understand what was happening. I didn't know what this was.

A game. A trick.

Real? A lie?

He let go of my arm, his hand clenched in a fist at his side. And I reached for the coffee, drinking it down in three big sips. It burned my mouth, but the pain cleared my head.

This was some new game, and I didn't know the rules.

I pulled my skirt back and stepped around him, a wide berth so no part of me brushed up against any part of him.

"Poppy," he breathed, and my name in his voice, that low timber, that dark accent, it held me like no grip on my elbow ever could. He didn't finish the statement, and I looked over at him.

His cold mouth was not folded in some charming smile. His eyebrow wasn't lifted in a sardonic curl. Everything about him was sharp.

"What?" I asked. For a moment, a razor-thin one, there was something he was going to say. I could feel it.

"No more drinking," he said, and just like that, he was gone.

Again.

By the time the lights dimmed and Caroline got up on the small stage to present me with the senator's award, I'd had two more champagne glasses. And, frankly, I was feeling all right. I should have been drunk at all these events. Justin came up beside me, and I wasn't sure how he managed to still look like someone's assistant in a thousand-dollar tux.

"Are you ready?" he whispered, pressing the neatly typed notes I'd approved a week ago into my hand.

"Sure," I said. How hard could this be? I'd done it a million times and, frankly, no one cared. I was doing it, and I didn't care.

"There are some changes," Justin said, and that jerked me into caring.

"What?"

"Caroline approved them." He pointed down

at the cards. I only had a second to look before Caroline on the stage was calling my name and smiling at me in the spotlight.

"I'm sure it's great," I said and lifted my skirt to climb the steps up to Caroline's side. There was a round of polite applause, and I was just drunk enough to wonder were they applauding my dead husband or me? Certainly not me. What had I ever done to earn applause?

"Thank you, Caroline," I said and took the small plaque she held out to me. I cradled it in my arms while lifting the notes so I could read them. The spotlight was blinding and hot, and I could feel a couple hundred eyes on me in a way that made my skin crawl.

Did they know? I wondered. That every single thing in my life was a lie?

"Poppy?" Caroline whispered, and I realized I was just standing there like a statue.

After clearing my throat, I read the notes— prattling on about the senator's commitment to struggling families. School lunch programs and affordable day care.

"But that was the senator's public life." This was new. All new. "In private, he was just as caring. Just as compassionate. Just as kind." These lies rattled me, and I felt an old coping mechanism slipping over me. The deep retreat into my body, where no one could touch me. Where no one could even *know* me. "All Jim wanted was to serve this great state and to have a family." My voice broke, and I looked at Caroline who only smiled at me, the way she usually did. Like she hadn't just driven over me with a Mack truck. "Unfortunately, in the brief time we were married, my pregnancies ended in miscarriage. And since he died before we could achieve one of those goals..." I kept reading, the words meaning nothing. They were new and not at all what I'd approved. And they split my private life right open. Part of me wanted to stop. But the lights and the eyes and the way I'd been trained for the last two years to never, ever make a fuss...

The words just kept coming.

We were creating a new foundation, Caroline and I. Better Families, Better New York. Millions of dollars to help struggling families in New York State.

I read off the card, and the crowd applauded, and Caroline was there taking the microphone away from me.

"What are you doing?" I asked her, baffled and shocked.

"Giving you purpose," she said and led me off the stage.

"All that stuff about Jim and me?" I asked when we were in the shadowed area beside the podium, and I could see Justin keeping people away from us. "That was private, Caroline."

"It's not private if everyone knows," she said, and I gasped, my hand against my stomach like she'd stabbed me.

"Poppy, this is the real world. And you've got to live in it. Come to my house tomorrow and we'll talk about everything."

And then . . . she was gone. And I was left bitter and fuming, holding a plaque with my abusive husband's name on it. Having told the whole room about my private heartbreak. And secret relief. A waiter walked by with an empty tray, and I put the plaque on it.

"Ma'am?" she asked.

"Throw it away. I don't care."

Another server came by with the champagne I needed, and I took two of them with me as I headed for the door. My purse, I thought, but didn't care. I wouldn't be touching up my makeup. And what did I need cash for? Nothing. I floated above cash. Above keys. It was just me and millions of dollars that I somehow kept selling my soul for. How many times could I do this to myself? For money I didn't care about? How many times could I just be a pawn in another person's game?

When was I going to grow a pair and figure out what I wanted?

"Poppy?"

It was Ronan, and there was a spark in me. A dangerous dark spark that even as it blazed I did my best to put out. That spark would only lead to humiliation. Embarrassment. Pain.

The first glass of champagne went down easily, and I just dropped the glass soundlessly on the carpet. The other glass I only drank half of it before doing the same. Wild, I felt wild. Just a breath away from being out of control, and I could sense him behind me. A heat. A force at my back.

Ignoring him was delicious.

I was electrified by his following me.

"Poppy," he said, and then once we were out of the ballroom he grabbed me by my elbow and pulled me down a darker hallway. I fought him, yanking my arm free, only to have him grab it harder in a grip that would leave a red mark on my skin.

I was an expert in such grips.

But still I kept fighting. If this guy was going to hit me, let him. Let him try and hurt me. There was nothing left of me to hurt.

"Poppy, goddamnit, stop," he said, and so fast he had a key out. He swiped it through a door, and we were in another room. A dark office with an empty desk. No windows.

All right. Now I was a little scared.

"What are you doing?" I asked, putting my hand over my elbow where he'd grabbed me.

"Did I hurt you?" he asked, watching me touch my skin. God. I not only felt outrageously alone with this man. I felt stupidly naked. This dress was nothing. Where was a suit of armor when you needed it?

I reached behind my back, pressing the doorknob lever, but he was there quick, putting his hand against the door right beside my head, keeping it shut. His breath stirred the small hairs escaping my too-tight bun.

The champagne only gave me so much courage, and I looked, not in his icy blue eyes but at his square chin with its five o'clock shadow. There was a scar there, just beneath his jaw line. It ran a straight line near his ear to nearly the point of his chin. Another jump from a window, I wondered. Or worse. Because Ronan seemed incredibly capable of worse.

"I'm going to ask you again," I said, my voice only a little shaky. "What are you doing?"

"Giving you a second to catch your breath," he said.

"Well, I was leaving, so why don't I just do that?"

He reached over and turned on a small lamp, the golden pool of light illuminated his face. And I'd talked to this man for what? A half hour, total in my life. A half hour over two and a half years. I owed him nothing. I pushed down the lever and pulled open the door.

"You're making a fool of yourself out there," he said, and I gasped in outrage, turning to face him.

"Fuck you."

"It's the truth. And you know it. You can't show them how much they're under your skin."

"What the hell do you know about anything?"

"I know I'm under your skin."

Said skin blazed hot and undoubtedly red. Right. This was the expected embarrassment. The humiliation right on cue. The ice cold look on his face melted and what was left was something so much worse. Something horrible.

Pity.

"Don't," I spat at him. "Don't look at me like that."

"Like what?" he asked.

"Like the rest of them look at me. Like all I am is something to be pitied and whispered about. Something to be used and shuffled around."

"I'm not—"

I shoved him. My hands against his rock-solid chest, and I shoved him. Hard enough he stepped backwards, and everything ignited in me. Everything. I looked at my hands, surprised they weren't flames.

He smiled, as if he could see the chemical reaction rippling through my body. And he liked it.

"I'm leaving," I said. Slightly scared of this. Slightly scared of myself. And him.

"You don't want to leave," he said, stepping closer, and the fire in my hands and my chest exploded between my legs. Desire like I'd never felt, like I'd never been allowed to feel fueled by rage and champagne and his Irish accent rippled all the way through me.

"You don't know a single fucking thing about me," I snarled.

"I know you don't want to be pitied. And I

know you just got fucked around pretty good up there in front of a thousand people."

I breathed hard through my nose.

"I think you want to fight," he said, a breath away from me. If I was another person I'd kiss him. Grab him by the silk lapels of his tux and pull that wicked mouth to mine. But I wasn't that person, for a million reasons. His eyes assessed me, and the longer I was silent, standing there burning and wretched, the pity came back.

"Or maybe I'm wrong about you," he said. "You don't have any fight in you. You are exactly what they made you." He reached for the door, and I knew he was going to let me go. Whatever test this was, I'd failed. "I'll make sure you get home."

I smacked him. I smacked him so hard my hand hurt. It burned and tingled. There was a print of my hand on his skin and that was the first time I'd ever done that, and part of me wanted to be horrified, but deep in my fully rioting soul, I was pleased.

So pleased.

The dark wing of his hair fell down over his eye, and he turned to face me, sweeping it back.

"There you go, Princess," he said. "That's what you need." He smiled at me like he suddenly recognized me as kin. Something long lost. But I felt undone. Incomplete. Something had started, a domino tipping over and setting off a chain reaction. And I needed him to complete it.

Or stop it.

Bursting right out of myself, I grabbed his lapels, pulling us into each other. Our bodies collided and sparked.

And I kissed him.

CHAPTER EIGHT

I T WAS THAT moment between action and reaction. The longest second in the world. Where there are a thousand different outcomes, and the universe was peeling its way through all of them. His lips against mine were open, like he was breathing me in, but he didn't kiss me.

He was just breathing. In and out. Against me.

I'd been a virgin on my wedding night. Something that seemed important to the senator. He'd touched the blood between my legs when the brief sex of our wedding night was over. He'd touched the blood and rubbed it between his fingers and said, in a satisfied way. "You're mine."

I'd been speechless with pain and disappointment, and so I said nothing, which was what he liked best, though I didn't know it at the time.

Before the senator there'd been a guy I worked with in the library in college. A boy in high school. But nothing prepared me for the senator, and nothing about the senator prepared me for Ronan.

For this feeling right now.

This ache. This need. I wanted him to *kis*s me.

"Poppy," he said, his voice a groan of regret. He was about to push me away. To end this.

So, I pulled him closer. Licked at his lips, waiting for him to snap or break. Push me away or kiss me back. Anything. Anything but this pitiful saying of my name.

His hands let go of the door and touched me. Feather-light like he was feeling his way across my back. I expected boldness from him. Wanted confident and sure and rough. I wanted him to be in control, and these careful touches weren't enough. Weren't nearly enough.

But I didn't know how to get more from him. How to incite him to more. How to ask for it.

He lifted his hands from my body, and I could feel him pulling away. "Ronan," I groaned, clinging to him. Trying to stop the inevitable.

And then suddenly he wasn't kissing me. He turned me away from him and pushed me up against the door. His body hot and hard against my back. Against my . . . ass. I could feel him there. Hard through his tuxedo pants. Proof he did want me. A shuddery relief went through me.

"What do you want, Princess?"

I pressed my forehead against the door and my ass against his cock and we both made a sound like we were being tortured. He cupped my breast in his wide rough palm.

"Say it," he groaned in my ear.

"I don't . . . I don't know."

His chuckle against my neck sent shockwaves through my body, and my knees buckled. He leaned harder against me, holding me between the door with is body. "I think you do," he said, his hands still. His hips still. "I think you know what you want. You're just too scared to say it."

I arched as best I could against him. I didn't know what to do. How to seduce a man. How to make him want me. I was clueless and stupid.

And still I wanted him to touch me.

"Don't you want me?" I whispered, hating the words. Hating myself for saying them.

"Why would I want you?" His words were a slap.

I went still, pulling myself deep inside my body. Where I couldn't be hurt.

"You're a pawn. A mouse," he whispered, and I pushed away from the door trying to get away from him and his hands, both of them came up to the bodice of my dress. Reaching between my skin and the silk to cup my naked skin in his hands. I gasped. Torn down the middle by his words and his actions. The silk of my dress tore as he shoved it down, baring my breasts to the cool air.

It was violent.

"What are you doing?" I whispered.

"Giving you what you want."

"Not . . . not like this."

I braced my hands against the door and shoved, but he put his mouth at my neck at the tender skin behind my ear and he bit me. I couldn't control the tortured moan in my throat. His mouth traveled down my shoulder, planting wet, open-mouthed kisses as he went. Sucking and biting, and I collapsed back against the door. I was angry? Why was I angry?

"You're scared of your shadow," he murmured, pulling the skirt of my dress up with one hand as his other cupped my breast, pulled my nipple taut until I cried out in pleasure and pain. This was too much. He was too much. I'd jumped into some kind of deep end with a man who disdained me, and I couldn't find the will to stop him.

Where was my pride?

"Do I want you?" he breathed as he slid his

hand down over the soaked satin of my barely-there thong. I shuddered and tried to escape, but he literally held me in the palm of his hand. I couldn't tell if he was being mean or sarcastic. I couldn't tell if he was playing a game or being honest. I didn't have the experience or the confidence to make sense of this.

I just knew that I wanted him. Mean, sarcastic, whatever I could get from him.

He pulled the wet satin out of his way, and then he was touching me where no one had touched me for years. *Years.* I'd even stopped touching myself. Sex was a chore. And no part of my body wanted it.

But now . . . oh my god now, my body wanted everything. Anything. Whatever dark depraved thing he wanted to do to me, I wanted it times ten. I couldn't breathe for the desire filling me. His fingers slipping over every inch of me, and I was on my tip toes, my head thrown back. I didn't care what he said. Or what he thought if he would just make me come.

So long, it had been so very, very long.

"Look at you." His voice was cold, and I whimpered. "So needy. So desperate." He said it like it was wrong. Gross.

"I'm sorry," I choked.

The hand that had been torturing my breasts came up to my throat, and he held me with my head arched back.

"For what?" he asked. "What are you sorry for?"

Wanting him so much. Being so needy.

Everything.

"I'll leave," I breathed. "Just let me go."

I whimpered as one long finger slid down over my clit. Pressing hard enough to fill my body with sparks.

"No," he groaned, and my knees gave out. He held me by my throat and the fingers inside of me. "It's too late for that."

"Then what do you want?" I twisted against his body. He was a silent steady pressure against my back.

"That girl at the party who was about to run off into the night. I want her. But she doesn't exist anymore, does she?"

I whimpered in pain. My soul. My body. Everything was hurt by his words.

His fingers against my clit were rough and hard, and no one had ever touched me that way so I had no idea how much I liked it. How his hand around my neck made me feel caught. I couldn't resist. I couldn't refuse.

All I could do was stand there and take the pleasure he was forcing on me.

"Oh, look at you," he said, his voice dark with disdain and desire. "Look at how you love it. What could I do to you?" he asked and licked my earlobe before sucking it into his mouth. "I could fuck you. Right here, couldn't I? Put you on your knees and feed you my cock until you couldn't breathe." All of it. He could do all of it. But I didn't have to say it. He felt it in my body. My total surrender. My breath was coming out in pants and moans, and I needed his fingers inside me. Inside. I was going to die if he didn't put something, anything inside me.

Two fingers pushed hard inside me, and I was shuddering. Sobbing. The orgasm I needed a breath away. Two.

"I could stop," he said, and he did. His fingers still inside me. His hand around my throat applied no pressure. I couldn't move. Push him away even.

But I didn't. I closed my eyes and tears rolled down my cheeks. I waited, but so did he.

"Jesus, Princess. If you want it, ask for it."

Like he knew how hard I'd been conditioned not to. How my self-denial was so deeply ingrained. "I promise you," he said. "I promise that girl in the ball gown cracking jokes, that if you just ask, if you just *say it*. I will give it to you."

"Please." It burst out of me with perfect manners. "Please, don't stop. Make me come. Please."

"There you go," he said, like he was proud of me, and his fingers were a madness inside my body. In my throat there was a keening sound I couldn't swallow and would embarrass me when I remembered it tomorrow. And I wanted him to pull up the back of my skirt and undo his pants. I wanted him inside my body in a way I'd never wanted anything ever before.

He wasn't doing it, so I tried to help it along. Pulling up my skirt, reaching behind me for his pants. The hard steel length of his cock in his pants.

"No." His hands left my body to slap my own hands against the wall. "Like this."

And I could have fought, but he'd already said it. I was a mouse. And I let him touch me the way he wanted. Hold me the way he wanted. Against this wall, my hair falling down my face like we were strangers. Animals.

I let him make me come in a wild ecstatic explosion of pleasure and pain. I cried. I might have screamed. I was light, and I was dust. And I was so far out of my body it was relief.

But I imagined all those things he said to me. I imagined him fucking me against this door, or the desk. I imagined the taste of him on my tongue.

I imagined . . . oh god . . . I imagined that savage mouth against mine.

The sweet violence of his kiss.

And I wanted him all over again. More, even, than before. It hurt how much I wanted his kiss.

It took me a moment to realize where he'd been a living breathing blanket damp with sweat against my back, there was only cool fresh air.

He wasn't holding my neck. His fingers were not between my legs.

Ronan wasn't touching me at all. I couldn't feel him even an inch away. On shaky legs I turned, my skirt falling back down to the floor, hiding the thong pulled to the side, my slick thighs. The mess he'd made of me.

He stood by the desk, his hands sweeping his dark hair away from his face. His fingers, I could see were wet from being inside my body. Wet from my come.

"Fix your dress, Poppy," he said.

"My . . . dress?" the words didn't make sense. Was it English? My brain had short-circuited.

He pointed at my chest, and I realized the bodice was gaping, revealing my breasts. The silk torn. "Cover yourself."

Another unwanted memory. The senator on our wedding night standing over the bed where I lay naked.

You're not much to look at, are you?

Shaking my head didn't change the memory. Or what had just happened here. I tugged the bodice up as best I could, holding my hands over my skin. Wishing I could cover myself.

This dress cost ten thousand dollars, and it was ruined. I felt ruined.

"You leave first. Go straight to your car. You look like you've been fucked against a wall."

I understood what was happening. The rejection. It had been inevitable, in a way. This was what I got for wanting something.

Anything.

But I was not a child on my wedding night. I was a woman who'd endured enough of a man's disdain.

"Fuck you," I said through gritted teeth and reached for the doorknob. He moved so fast I didn't get it open before he was right in front of me again. His fingers cupping my face.

"Keep your blood up. You're going to need it.

Be smart. Now, go."

I jerked my head out of his grip and was out that door like an Irish devil was on my heels. But of course, when I turned at the end of the hallway, he wasn't there.

I had no idea where my purse was, so I left it and my phone, and I stepped out onto the windy 27th street and, like magic, there was my car. My driver. My life operating as it always had.

When I felt somehow . . . changed.

"Ma'am?" my driver said. The wind whipped his coat away from his body, lifted his pale hair off his head.

"Yes?" We stood by the open door. A storm was blowing in from someplace.

"Are you all right?" he asked. He had a nice face my driver. And he was younger than I thought.

So much sudden concern from the men in my life.

"I think so. Yes," I said and climbed into the back seat. He slammed the door behind me and then we were pulling away from the curb. The party.

The car ride home I spent squashing the lingering fires in my body. Distancing myself from the memory of his fingers around my throat. The open-mouthed kisses on my neck. I pushed them away and framed them up like they weren't my memories. It was exactly what I did to survive being married to Jim. They were a book I read. Or a movie I saw.

The shame of having to do it again was unwanted, so I turned it into anger.

And I seethed with that anger all the way up to Bishop's Landing.

The house was dark. And I was alone. The alarm beeped as I entered the front door, and I punched in the code to make it stop.

Theo, the driver, lived in the cottage at the end of the property. Jim's bodyguard was no longer around. It was just me and seven empty bedrooms. An office wing. A formal dining room. Eight and a half baths.

There was so much room, and I rattled around inside it like a lost toy.

In the dark I went to the drink cart in the sitting room, and I poured myself a glass of something that burned as I shot it back. I poured myself another one and took off my light-as-air, pencil-thin Jimmy Choo stilettos and walked barefoot with my drink through the kitchen and the sliding glass door to the pool deck. Another drink and with nowhere to put the glass I heaved it at the far end of the patio stones where it smashed spectacularly.

Tonight . . . tonight had to be the end of something. Or the beginning. The way Caroline changed the speech. The way I came apart in Ronan's hands only to be tossed aside the second he'd taken me apart. I was being used by everyone. Enough.

I lit a fire in the small fire pit I'd made out of bricks and stone, and I took off the dress and the thong and naked in the moonlight I burned them.

Shivering, I watched my old life burn.

My blood was up. And I was ready for a fight.

CHAPTER NINE

T HE NEXT MORNING, my head pounding from my night of fury drinking, I walked the two miles over the ridge from my house to the giant Constantine compound on the very top of the hill. The 300-year-old mansion was known as The Queen of Bishop's Landing. Originally an apple orchard and farm, the land got sold bit by bit, but the house never changed hands. Hundreds of years of Constantine matriarchs and patriarchs, adding wings and electricity. Bathrooms and theaters. Tennis courts. Guard houses. Swimming pools. Manicured gardens. Helicopter pad.

Since the last troubles with the Morellis, it had been heavily guarded with armed men on the various balconies and in guard houses along the long driveway. Winston had bought the houses closest to the compound, so for a mile in every direction it was Constantine land.

My parent's old house was part of that. The willow tree and pond.

Rumor was that the Morellis used to have a house on this hill. I didn't know if that was true or not.

It was damp in the early sunlight, and the fog clung to the hedgerows and the tall trees. Despite the compound and the bulldozing of houses, most of Bishop's Landing was still forested.

I walked the overgrown path up the hill. The turret on the Constantine mansion was obscured by mist. I bypassed the driveway and used the old wooden gate built in the side of the fence set deeper in the woods. Mom showed us this fence when Zilla and I were girls, when we were in and out of this house like it was our own. I hadn't used it in years. But this morning, in my muddy Wellingtons and bedraggled ponytail—it seemed right.

I knocked on the door and squeezed the water out of my hair, waiting for one of the maids to answer.

"Poppy!" It was Denise. My favorite. She'd been around the longest and remembered my mother. "Ms. Constantine didn't tell me she was expecting you."

"She told me to come by last night."

"Did you make an appointment?"

"Nope," I said, stepping inside the foyer. I

wiped off my boots on the rug. I liked Denise, but I wasn't going to be sent away. "Is she in her office?"

"Yes," Denise said. "But why don't you let me—"

"I know the way, Denise. It's fine." I gave her a blinding smile. The kind of smile I gave servers and photographers when they noticed a bruise on my wrist and their eyebrows went up. It was my *no further questions* smile.

Caroline's office was up in the turret. And I took the wide sweeping center staircase up to the second floor and then the smaller staircase to the third, and in the corner by the old nursery and the maid's quarters was the final staircase up to her throne.

Justin had a desk at the top of the stairs. "Poppy!" he cried as he stood. "You don't have an appointment." He looked down at his desk like this unexpected interruption was going to send the whole house of cards to the floor.

"You're right," I said and pushed my way into Caroline's office anyway, right past him. The room was windowed on three sides, and the ceiling was gorgeous refurbished mahogany. All the décor cream, white, and gold with accents of pale pink.

In the middle of the room, standing opposite her desk was a man with his back to me in a black suit. I knew in a heartbeat who he was.

Ronan.

I had not anticipated him. And my body lurched with memory and shame. The urge to run was not small, but I stood there. I stood there, and I folded up those conflicting memories and I put them away. I wasn't stupid. And I wasn't a little girl. It was time for me to stop acting like I was.

And more importantly it was time to stop being distracted by what he did to me.

Who is he? I wondered. And how did he get so close to Caroline? So fast? That office in her building that I'd been sure was for family; it was clearly his. Which meant he was deeply inner circle.

"Poppy?" Caroline asked, looking around Ronan to see me in the doorway. Her eyes went wide at the way I was dressed. Jeans and wet hair, muddy boots. An old raincoat I found in the gardener's closet. "Are you all right?"

At that, Ronan turned, his face registering nothing. Not surprise or happiness or anger or disdain. Not even the memory of my ass grinding against his cock as I came so hard I left my body.

Nope. Ronan stared at me like we were strangers. And that was just great with me.

He'd worked some magic on me last night. Not just my body, but in my head, too. Pushing me out of that trap I'd lived in, too terrified to ask for what I wanted in fear of it being taken away.

Too terrified to want anything.

I felt stronger for having asked for something, even if it was something as strange as that man's hands on my body. Even if getting what I wanted sent me someplace dark and shameful.

Sex was so easy for some people. Why was it always a Greek tragedy for me?

"I'm fine," I said. "I was hoping we could talk?" My gaze flicked to Ronan, and I took great pleasure in sniffing dismissively. "Alone."

"Of course," she said. As she stood, she nodded at Ronan who turned and walked for the door. Brushing so close to me I could see that scar under his neck. I watched him go, all but daring him to look at me.

Of course, he didn't. Because in the end, I was a senator's widow, the good friend of his boss, and he was the help.

Now who is the coward? I thought. But didn't necessarily feel better for the thought.

The door closed behind him, and Caroline

gestured to the ivory chairs in front of her desk.

"You're mad at me," she said.

"I am," I said. "Those things you changed in the speech—"

"The new foundation was something your husband and I were working on. He signed the papers just a few nights before . . ." she trailed off.

"He put a bullet in his own head?" The crassness was a surprise. It was shades of my sister coming out, and I understood how delicious it could be to be irreverent. To say what I wanted.

"I was going to say ended his life, but okay, we can go your way."

"I'm not upset about the foundation." I crossed my legs, my muddy boots dripping on the floor. That, too, felt good. "You know what he did to me. How he treated me."

She nodded carefully.

"Then why make me lie about what a kind and decent man he was?"

"Because we wanted those people to donate money, and if you didn't put an end to the rumors—"

"Rumors?"

Her level gaze met mine, and I saw the pity, and I could not sit there and bathe in it.

I stood up, and she grabbed my hand.

"You were so young and everyone knew the situation with Zilla and your father," she said quickly, as if she were apologizing. But Caroline didn't do that. "You put up a good front," she said. "No one ever suspected how bad it was."

"Is that supposed to comfort me?"

"Yes."

"Well, it's crappy comfort. People knew he hurt me. They just didn't know how bad it was? *So* comforting." *Oh god, sarcasm. Who the hell was I?*

I looked at her, hard in the eyes, remembering how she turned me away. How she told me I needed to make it work. And I owed her a lot, but not this. Not anymore.

"I'm not doing that again," I said. "I'm done lying about him. About my marriage."

Caroline put her hands up. "I understand, and I won't ask that of you again. Okay?"

"Okay." I nodded like we'd signed a deal, and Caroline sat back, eyeing me with a careful smile.

"It wasn't kind of me to put you on the spot like that. But I knew if we'd run that by you—"

"I wouldn't have done it?" I interrupted.

"No. You would have. But you would have spent two weeks thinking about it. Hurting yourself with it."

That was undoubtedly true.

"Don't be angry with me, Pops," she said. "I was only trying to do what had to be done. You understand that, don't you?"

"Yes," I said because what else was I going to do? Hold a grudge? Against Caroline? Impossible. She smiled, sitting back in her seat.

"But you have to understand that it's different now. I'm different."

Caroline shook her head at me, a smile spreading across her face. "God, your mother would be so proud of you right now."

The compliment stroked me like nothing else in the world could. "I suppose it's about time," I said.

"I'd say."

"So?" I said. "Are you going to tell me about this foundation we've started?"

"Yes." She checked her watch and stood up. "But I have to go into the city for a meeting. I'll have Justin send over the details. Jim signed the paperwork before he died. You can step in as executive director as soon as you're ready."

"Executive director?" I said, stunned.

"Why not?"

"Because I have zero experience."

"You worked for Jim's foundation." She

shrugged.

"Yeah, as like a glorified fundraiser."

"That's not true," Caroline said. "You had big plans."

"Caroline," I said and shook my head. They were hardly big plans. It was an idea that with enough money we could solve small problems. Make big changes in small ways. Micro-loans for single mothers. Breakfast programs for smaller school districts. Rural bus route improvements. Fidget toys for diagnostic kindergartens. Classroom wish lists for public school teachers. The kinds of programs that weren't sexy and didn't make the news, but that would really matter.

"They were creative, and you are capable. I'll be right behind you making sure nothing goes wrong. But I have total faith in you."

Total faith. Had anyone ever had total faith in me? Had *I* ever had total faith in me?

I got to my feet. "Monday?" I asked.

"Do you feel like you're ready to go to work?"

"Past ready. But—" I was really feeling myself here.

"You want to negotiate salary?"

"No." I didn't need money. I had more money than I knew what to do with. "But you're not lying to me anymore, Caroline. I'm not a pawn you can push around to get what you want. I owe you so much, but I don't owe you my pride anymore."

She looked at me for a long time, completely unreadable. And then she smiled, not the soft fuzzy one I usually got, but the one she saved for her bloodthirsty children.

"What's gotten into you?" she asked.

"I don't actually know," I said. But Ronan was the answer. Ronan and burning my clothes.

"Well, I like it. When you're ready, call me."

On the tip of my tongue was a question about Ronan, about who he really was and why she trusted him, but she was all but pushing me out the door. And I didn't know how to ask about Ronan without giving everything away. Every conflicted feeling I was wrestling with when it came to him.

Just *thinking* his name made me blush.

There were moments last night when I hated him as much as I ever hated Jim. But I never wanted a man the way I wanted Ronan.

No man had ever made me so curious. Or reckless.

And the way he seemed to know the power of asking for what I wanted? What was I supposed to do with that kind of man?

"The foundation's offices are in the Halcyon building. When you're ready, we will get you all set up."

I wondered briefly why the offices weren't in the brownstone, but in the end it didn't matter. My future was happening.

There was a memory, dim and fragmented, of my two years at college. How I'd ridden my bike around Union, feeling that excited . . . possibility. This feeling in my chest didn't feel like that, but I wasn't a girl anymore.

That excitement was behind me. But maybe I had a chance at being useful again. At doing something good. And if I wasn't excited, I was challenged. Interested. Ready.

From Caroline's office I went down all the stairways and out the side door. I passed a dozen servants as I went, each of them smiling and following me with their eyes like I'd done something suspicious. Outside the sun was burning off the fog, and I walked across the lawn to the treeline and the small gate that I'd used to get here.

At the sight of a man standing there, I stopped, apprehensive. *What was the deal with all this security?* I wondered. But then I realized it was Ronan, and my apprehension morphed into something far more complicated. Fear and anger and a desire so strong I felt drunk.

"This is how you got through all the security?" he asked, pushing the wooden gate open and closed. The squeal of its rusty hinges startled birds from the forest behind him.

"How'd you find it?"

He gestured behind me, my dark tracks in the dew spangled grass. "Well, congratulations," I said. "You caught me infiltrating the compound. Whatever will you do with me?"

He licked his upper lip in a move that was so outrageously sexy, so . . . dirty, I felt my nipples harden under the baggy coat I wore.

"You got a mouth on you," he said.

The better to bite you with, I thought but definitely didn't have the balls to say. "What do you want?"

He lifted his eyes.

"You forgot something at the gala," he said.

My pride?

He held out my clutch. The dark indigo silk beautiful against his skin and the white of his shirt. I took it, careful not to touch him, but he held onto it for a second.

"Poppy," he said.

"What?"

All that deadly stillness, that careful practiced impenetrable mask he wore every time I saw him since that first meeting here, two years and a lifetime ago, it dropped, and I recognized the beaten, slightly baffled man I'd met in the shadows. The man who wasn't sure why he was here, or who he was supposed to be inside this house.

You, I thought. *I recognize you.*

"You need to be careful, Princess," he said.

"Of you? Lesson learned."

He tugged on the purse, and I fell off balance towards him. My body collided with his, and I gasped, affronted and unimpressed by his little tricks.

But also stupidly turned on.

"I'm not what's coming through your door."

"You're not coming through anything of mine," I snapped back at him, and his lips curled, heat settling between us.

"Sweetheart," he whispered, his breath against my mouth. "If I came through your door, we both know you'd spread your legs for me so fast—"

I grabbed the purse and shoved away from him.

"I survived the monster under my bed," I said. "And I'm rich now, or haven't you heard?"

"Your money won't keep you safe," he said. "And there is more than one monster in Bishop's Landing."

"Who are you?" I asked.

"I'm no one, Princess. I've told you that."

"I'm not a fool, Ronan. You were at my house. You talked to the senator. You're living in Caroline's pocket. Who. Are. You?"

He stepped closer, and I stood my ground, not about to cower. Those days were over.

"Try it, asshole. See what happens," I growled at him, and his eyes opened wide for a second as if surprised. As if impressed.

"I'm no one," he said again. "You need to concentrate on your own life."

"You need to fuck off."

He was repeating himself, and if he wasn't going to bring something new to our conversation I was done. Done with him. Done with who he'd turned me into. The gate was cockeyed and open, and I pushed past him and slipped between it and the fence heading into the forest, down the trail back to my house.

I didn't turn around despite the fact I could feel the burn of his gaze on the bare skin of my neck. That had to win me some points, right?

One thing was clear—he was the danger.

Ronan was the unknown. The new monster in my life. And I'd learned some valuable lessons from my last one. Information was key. I wouldn't be walking into anything blindly. Not again.

Once I was out of sight of the compound, I opened my purse and pulled out my phone.

Four texts from Zilla. A missed call. I had enough battery left to call her back.

"Hey!" She answered halfway through the first ring, and it did not escape me that our roles for the moment were reversed. "You had me worried."

"Sorry, I left my phone at a gala. I just got it back."

"A gala," she said. "Sounds awful."

"It was. It really . . . was."

"What's wrong, Poppy?"

I bit my lip and stared up at the sky. This was a big dangerous step. "If you needed to find out something about a Constantine, how would you find it?"

"None of this sounds like a good idea."

"There's a guy working for Caroline, and I just need to know his story."

"Have you tried asking him?"

"You're hilarious." This was crossing a line; I was well aware of that. But I couldn't live like this anymore. The girl left in the dark. And I couldn't wait for people to decide to tell me what I needed to know.

I had to get my own answers.

"Well, you won't like my answer," Zilla said.

"What would you do?"

"Call a Morelli."

"I don't know any," I said.

"I do. But, Poppy, are you sure you want to do this? You might start another Morelli and Constantine war, and you'll be right in the middle of it."

"Zilla," I said, stepping through the tall grass. I hit the top of the hill. The senator's house . . . *my* house, down below. "I don't have that kind of power."

"Well, you've never been a good judge of how much power you have, Poppy. But stay by your phone. I'll be in touch."

CHAPTER TEN

"ANOTHER?" THE BARTENDER at the Red Hook dive bar asked me. He had a t-shirt on with the sleeves cut out. I could see his armpit hair. It was revolting. And fascinating.

"No, thank you," I said, thinking I needed to be on top of my game. Whatever game that was. One very cheap Pinot Grigio was all I was going to have before meeting my sister's mysterious Morelli.

This was a bad idea. I could see that from my vantage spot on this hard stool in this shabby bar. But since the second I decided to find out what I could about Ronan, I'd been obsessed. What happened the night of the gala had been running through my mind on a loop, forcing me to live in this sort of anguished, disbelieving and constantly turned-on place.

And I didn't know a single thing about the guy other than how his hand felt against my throat. What his voice sounded like in my ear.

How his wrist felt against the bare skin of my belly.

Sex wasn't something I thought about. Not for a long, long time. And now, the brush of my clothes against my skin put me on edge. The seam of my jeans between my legs had me halfway to orgasm. I wanted to forget everything he did to me. But I replayed every moment like my sister played Pink's Greatest Hits when she was eleven. Nonstop.

"You want food or something?" the bartender asked, sliding a plastic menu at me. He could not seem less invested in me wanting food.

"I'm fine. I'm just meeting someone."

"Whatever," he said and turned back to the baseball game playing on the television over the bar.

I'd never been in a bar like this. Sticky floor. Neon signs. There were bowls of peanuts, and people just threw the shells on the floor. It was unhygienic, disrespectful, and dangerous for people with allergies and . . . amazing.

All these people who just did not give a shit? I mean . . . I didn't want to know them, but it was fun to see it happening.

Zilla had told me to dress down. To try and not stand out, so I wore jeans I hadn't worn in years and a sweatshirt from Union College, my alma mater. My hair was back in a ponytail, and I had no makeup on my face. Not even mascara. I found an old pair of Converse tennis shoes in the back of my closet from my days before Jim, and they fit just like they used to.

I felt like a kid doing something really wrong.

And I kind of liked it.

The bell over the door rang out, and the bartender looked over and threw his hands up in the air.

"No way, man," he said. "Again?"

I turned as a man walked in wearing a suit and a do-not-fuck-with-me expression. His silence was seriously the most threatening thing I'd ever experienced, and he just stared at the bartender and his armpit hair.

"Everyone clear out," the bartender finally shouted. People ignored him until he brought his fingers to his lips and split the air with a whistle that got everyone's attention. "I said get out."

I'd already paid my bill, so I grabbed my purse and went to walk out with everyone else. Was it some political thing? Was the president coming in? Oh my god, was it the mob? It hardly mattered, I was just happy to get out of this suddenly tense bar. But the silent man at the door stopped me. "Not you," he said and pointed me back towards the bar stool I'd just left.

"But—" I looked up at his face and shut up. This unassuming man was nothing but dark inside. Dead. His eyes were reptilian. A chill ran down my spine.

I turned and sat back down on my stool.

"You know every time this shit happens, I lose thousands of dollars," the bartender said.

"Abe," a woman said as she came walking in the door. If I was dressed down, she was dressed to the nines. A fur coat and long dark brown hair. Diamonds in her ears, more on her fingers. Leopard print Louboutins. "Every time this shit happens, I pay you more than this place makes in a year."

"It's the principal, Eden."

"It's a shithole, Abe."

"Well, it's my shithole. And I've got some pride."

"Here." Eden made her way over to the bar and pulled from her Coach+Billy Reid Crocodile Tote a stack of bills and put it on his bar. "That should help with the pride. And bring me a bottle of whatever passes for vodka back there."

Abe rolled his eyes but pocketed the bills and brought over to where I was sitting a bottle of

Grey Goose and two rocks glasses filled with ice. He set them on the bar, and I sat back like they were alive and going to bite.

So, clearly, I'd made a few mistakes in asking for this meeting.

"Thank you, Abe," she said in a sing song voice as she walked across the bar to me. Prowled really. I felt like I was being stalked by some jungle cat.

This was my sister's Morelli. She had the signature dark looks and the same frantic energy just under her skin. The same fuck-you-world way of moving through a place. The fur coat parted as she walked, sliding down over a shoulder. The mink grazing across the floor, through the peanut shells.

I winced on the mink's behalf.

"You look like a tourist," the woman said. Eden? That was what the bartender called her.

"I've never been here," I said with a shrug.

"No shit." The skintight black dress poured over her impressive Morelli curves and ended at the very tops of her legs. She was sex walking, and I felt stupid in my jeans. In my body.

She walked past me to the jukebox in the corner, and I swivelled on my stool to watch her. It felt dangerous to take my eyes off her.

She held out her hand towards me.

"Quarter?" she said, still looking at the juke-box.

"I . . . ah . . . I don't have any change."

"Jacob?" Eden said, and the man standing at the door put a hand in his pocket and pulled out some change. He walked across the room and put a quarter in her palm. "You like Dolly?" she asked.

I glanced at dead-inside Jacob and then looked for Abe who wasn't behind the bar.

"Are you talking to me?"

"Oh my god, honey, yes. I am talking to you. And now you don't get a vote."

Eden punched the buttons with a lot of enthusiasm, and within minutes *Jolene* was coming through the speakers.

"You know, if I wrote music," Eden said turning away from the jukebox. "I would write a song called Dolly entirely from Jolene's point of view and it would be like, why do you want such a shit guy? If I can take him, just because I can, don't you think it's worth looking for some other dude?"

Eden sat on the chair next to me. Her knee hitting mine. Her fur slipping over my leg.

"I don't honestly understand why no one has

done that yet," she said, looking at me with her eyebrows up.

"Me neither," I said, having given this question zero thought.

"You must be Poppy," she said, filling each glass with Grey Goose. She picked hers up and held it out for a cheers. But I didn't pick mine up. This was all moving a little too fast. She tapped the edge of her glass against mine before draining hers. "You don't look at all like those pictures of you in the news."

"No?" I asked, oddly curious if this was a good thing or a bad thing.

"You look like a human. In the news you looked like a paper doll."

I laughed.

"Did I say something funny?"

"I was a paper doll. Exactly a paper doll."

"What can I say? I've got a way with words. You going to drink with me, or what?" She picked up my glass and all but put it in my hands. "Cheers Big Ears," she said and touched her glass to mine and shot down another glass full of vodka. I took a sip and attempted to set down my glass, but she put her fingers against the bottom of it. Tipping the glass so I had to drink or it would spill all over.

"Good girl," she said as I gasped and wiped my face.

"In any case," she refilled our glasses. "I'm sorry for your loss. I always thought the senator seemed like a good guy."

"He wasn't," I said without thinking. The vodka and her boldness making a mess of me. Immediately I regretted giving her that information.

"No?" She smiled at me. Like a snake. "In what way?"

"In every way," I said.

"Isn't that interesting? Though, probably not so much for you. How long were you married?"

"Two years. But we're not here to talk—"

"You had two miscarriages? Sorry. That's not easy."

"How do you know that?" The first miscarriage was pretty public. The second one not so much.

"You think I'm going to show up without knowing who I'm meeting?" she asked like I was stupid, and maybe I was. Because I knew nothing about her.

"You're Eden Morelli?" I asked, trying to somehow get on the offensive in this strange conversation.

"In the flesh." She did a flourish with her hand. The diamonds on her fingers flashing in the low light.

"Who . . . who is that guy?" I asked, turning to look at the bodyguard at the door. Watching us with his dead eyes.

"Jacob?" she said. "You don't need to worry about him. Former military." Eden leaned in conspiratorially. "Secret ops. After the last Morelli Constantine dustup, I got myself the best bodyguard available on the dark web."

Every single word in that sentence was terrifying.

"I'm not . . . a threat . . . to you," I said, because I was scared of Jacob. And Eden, frankly. "I just wanted some information."

Eden flipped her dark hair over her shoulder, her green eyes glittering. "Like you don't know information is the most dangerous threat there is." She lifted her glass again. "One more. Your sister was right about you."

"What did she say?"

"That you used to be fun. Now you act like you're allergic."

"I'm not allergic," I said, wounded. "Just out of practice."

"Well, I'm a hell of a coach, let's go."

With the last shot of vodka warming me up from the inside, I picked up my glass and took a sip, which seemed to be enough for Eden Morelli.

"Your sister said you wanted some dirt on one of Caroline's employees?"

"Yeah. A guy named Ronan."

"You know. You're pretty tight with the Constantines, seems that maybe just asking Caroline might be easier."

"That's not a good idea," I said, trying to keep it vague, but it felt like I was spilling my guts about everything. This woman was watching me so carefully it was like she could see the things I wasn't saying. "I don't even know his last name."

"Byrne," she said. *Ronan Byrne.* Yeah. That felt . . . right.

"You know him?"

"Only by reputation and what I've been able to find out. Which isn't much."

"What is his reputation?" I asked.

"Well, no one would ever confuse him for a good guy."

I did. That night at my engagement. And perhaps . . . perhaps at the fundraiser. Before he said all those things to me. Before he pushed me away like I was trash. Before he made me feel like trash.

"Well, his childhood is a whole Charles Dickens thing. Mom wasn't around. Dad was in and out the army and jail. Died when he was about ten. Ronan grew up in a protestant boarding school. He has more hospital records than anything else."

"Hospital?"

"Someone liked beating the shit out of him."

I took a sip of vodka, the glass cold against my lips as that information sunk in.

"How did Caroline find him?"

Eden shrugged. "The Constantines have had their fingers in the oil drilling off the coast of the UK for a couple of decades. She could have met him at any point."

"But why is he here? Now?"

"A good junkyard dog can be hard to find," Eden said, tilting her head back towards Jacob by the door. I flinched at her language. "Too real for you, Poppy?" She said my name with all the p sounds.

"Ronan's not a bodyguard," I said. I really didn't think he was. Caroline still had the same armed guards she always had. With the earpieces and the triangle formation around her.

No, Ronan was something else. Something closer. Something more trusted. He had an office outside her door. He was in her home on the weekend.

"And why would he come here?" I was thinking out loud. That night I met him. He'd been beaten up and slightly baffled. He didn't know why he was there. At that party. In the States.

I haven't been invited in yet.

"Money talks," Eden said. "And some guys like having a reason to be . . . unleashed. The Constantines and Morellis don't have much in common, but they can offer a certain kind of person a . . . certain kind of pleasure."

That whole sentence made my skin crawl. But part of it rang me like a bell. The truth could be so undeniable.

"How do you know Zilla?" I asked. Behind Eden, Jacob's head snapped our way, and something awful curled in my stomach. *Oh, Zilla. What have you been up to?*

My sister wanted to be unleashed. That was what her manic side craved. A lawless state where she was judge, jury, and executioner. And something sparked in Jacob's dead eyes at the mention of my sister's name.

"Zilla and I go way back," Eden said. She drained the last of the vodka and stood up, the fur coat slipping off her shoulder. And that was suddenly the end of the conversation. "I'm sorry that's all I know. Ronan Byrne is a bit of a ghost." And if she was drunk from the half a bottle Grey Goose she'd just shot down, she didn't show it. "So? About my payment?"

"How much?" I asked, reaching for my bag. Zilla had not mentioned payment, but nothing was free. I knew that better than most.

"Oh honey. Money is so Constantine. The Morellis deal in something else entirely."

She stepped forward, far too close. We'd shifted while talking, and I'd turned towards her. Suddenly, she was between my thighs. Her bare skin pressed up against my jeans. I could smell the vodka. The Jardin d'Amalfi she wore. A cigarette she might have smoked before coming in. Her eyes were dilated, and I wondered what else was in her system outside the vodka.

"What do you want?" I asked. "If not money."

"Lots of things," she said, and her finger lightly touched the side of my face. I could not mistake her intent.

"I won't . . . have sex with you."

"Well, that's too bad. You were growing on me." She stepped back, tugged her fur coat up around her body. "We'll do this the old-fashioned way, I guess. You owe me one."

"One what?"

"Favor." She picked her purse up from the bar. "Relax. I'm not going to ask you to kill anyone. Probably." She winked and turned for the door. "But if you want my advice, stay away from Ronan Byrne. The ones who have spent their life fighting don't know when to stop."

A favor? I thought in the car on the way back from Red Hook to Bishop's Landing. What in the world could I offer a person like Eden Morelli? I didn't know anything. I had no political secrets. And I didn't know anything about the Constantines that she didn't know. What if she wanted me to spy?

Well, she would be disappointed, in the end.

Theo pulled up to the front of the house, and I opened the door before he got there to open it for me. Stepping out of the car, I caught his rather stunned expression.

"I think I'd like to learn how to drive," I said. For the brief period of time between my father's death and the evaporation of all our money and resources and my marriage to the senator, I rode a bike around campus or took Ubers.

Not being able to drive had kept me captive, in a way. Relying on Theo, when if I'd been able to drive, maybe I would have made a break for it on my own.

No. I wouldn't have.

But driving would be part of my new independence.

"Ma'am?" Theo said.

"Will you teach me?" I asked, and the poor guy blanched, looking around like he had to check with someone before saying anything. And maybe it was the vodka, or maybe it was brushing up against Eden Morelli who so clearly lived her life on her own terms, but I was done living my life like the senator was still alive.

I wasn't a paper doll. Not anymore.

"The senator is dead. He doesn't decide what happens in this house anymore."

Theo blinked like I'd said something he wasn't expecting. Well, he'd better get used to it. I was just starting to be unexpected.

"I can teach you," Theo said.

"Good." I walked past him into my dark house.

I opened the front door and punched in the code to the alarm to make it stop beeping. In the dark, I walked down the hallway past the rooms I never used and was never going to, the sitting room and the study with the fireplace that had not seen a fire once in the two years I lived here.

In the kitchen, I got a glass of water and drank it down.

Did Eden Morelli really hit on me? Did that actually happen?

Laughing, I filled up my empty glass and took it up the stairs to my bedroom. My bedroom was all white, as per the senator's request. Floors, ceiling, linens. The furniture was mahogany and dark in the shadows.

I hated all white.

I should change it.

"I should move," I said out loud.

"And go where, Princess?"

I screamed, dropped the glass and fumbled for the light, but he crept out of the shadows before I could turn it on.

"Leave it," Ronan said. "This is a conversation better suited to the dark."

CHAPTER ELEVEN

HEART POUNDING, THE vodka in my stomach churning, I ran.

I made it down the hallway to the top of the stairs before he grabbed my hand, yanking me to a halt so fast it wrenched my shoulder.

"What the hell are you doing in my house?" I cried, trying to get my hand free, but his grip was iron. And I knew when I couldn't win against a man's strength. So I stopped fighting and waited for him to relax.

"I'm here to get some questions answered," he said, turning back to the bedroom, pulling me behind him like a fish.

Yeah, I wasn't going back into that bedroom with him. I started fighting again. If I could get downstairs to the alarm—

"Stop it, Poppy," he growled and grabbed me by the waist and hauled me back into the bedroom. He threw me down on the bed, and I scrambled off, standing on the other side of it. In front of me was the king-size bed, Ronan, and a dozen yards between me and the door.

Behind me were French doors and a balcony. If I was careful and did everything just right when I jumped, I would land in the pool.

"Thinking of jumping out that window?" he asked. "I wouldn't. It would be a shame to end this night scraping your broken body off the deck."

"What do you want?" I asked, taking a step backwards towards the door.

"To talk some sense into you."

"In my bedroom?"

"Calm down, Poppy. I'm not going to hurt you."

I made some kind of scoffing whimpering noise in my throat and took another tiny step back.

"You don't believe me?" He circled the bed, and there was no place for me to go but back against the wall. "You think I already hurt you?"

He made it sound like I was a child. Like I had no idea all the ways he could give me pain.

"Stop." I put up my hand, as if I could fend him off.

He grabbed me by the elbows, yanking me up on my toes. "How am I supposed to keep you safe when you do something as stupid as go talk to the Morellis?"

The moonlight caught him across the face, and I'd never seen him so angry.

"Keep me safe?" I laughed, which was probably risky considering his anger. But I was beyond giving a shit. Those words didn't even make sense coming from him.

"What did you talk to Eden Morelli about?" he asked.

"How do you even know I did?"

"There are a thousand wires crisscrossing between the Morellis and the Constantines, and you tripped half of them reaching out to Eden. Who, just to be clear, is not to be taken lightly. She's as bad as they get. Feral, like. Vicious."

"And what are you?"

"Oh, Princess, I think I've been very good to you." The low purr of his voice thrummed between us. Making the memory of his hands between my legs tangible and real.

It was time for this to be over. I pushed at his chest, but he didn't budge. If anything, he pulled me closer. My toes barely touching the floor. But I didn't wince. Or beg. I gave him nothing.

"Am I hurting you?" he breathed.

"You know you are."

"This is nothing compared to what could be done to you."

"You think I don't know?" I spat at him. "You think there's one inch of pain you can show me that I don't know by heart?"

His eyes were dark in the shadows, all the color leached from his body. He was black and white and grey. But when he smiled, he gleamed.

"There you are," he said. God, this man. He was only happy when I was spitting at him.

"What do you want?" I asked. "What do I need to do to get you out of here?"

The grandfather clock in the hallway clicked forward a minute, so loud in the quiet between us.

"What would you do?" His voice was soft.

"Not what you're thinking."

"You don't have the slightest idea what I'm thinking."

I rolled my eyes at him. Something that once got me smacked so hard I had to go to the dentist. "Trust me, Ronan. You're not as original as you think you are."

That made him tip back his head and howl with laughter, and then he stepped away, slowly letting go of my body which I let sag against the wall while I caught my breath. Pretending to be brave. Strong. It took a lot of effort. Far more effort than cowering and hiding. But I was done cowering and hiding.

He pulled a chair that usually sat beside the dresser forward to sit directly across from me. "What are you doing?"

"Sitting down. You're going to answer a few questions for me."

"I'm not going to do shit for you."

"Swear to god, Poppy. You're making this harder than you need to."

"Good."

In the shadows I watched him look up at the ceiling, a hard sigh. A throbbing heartbeat in his throat. "You called the fucking Morellis," he said. "If you're foolish enough to think that nothing bad was going to come of it, you're wrong. I'm here. I'm the bad that comes of it, Poppy. You'll be answering some questions."

"Fine," I said. Because he wasn't wrong. The only place for me to sit was the bed, and that wasn't going to happen. So, I stayed on my feet but didn't lean against the wall. I was getting tiny little points in tiny little ways. "Ask your questions."

"Why did you go to the Morellis?"

"To get information."

"On Caroline?"

That made me blink. "No. Why would I want information on Caroline?"

"The senator?" He began tapping the arm of the chair with his middle finger. A small sign of impatience.

"No. I know everything I need to know about the senator."

"The foundation?" The foundation? I felt a strange chill. What didn't I know about the foundation?

"You," I said, tired of the guessing. "I went to the Morellis to get information about you."

His finger stopped tapping on the chair.

"What did you want to know about me?" he asked, his voice terrifyingly careful.

"Who you are? Where you came from? Why Caroline trusts you so much? So fast?"

"You didn't need to go to a Morelli for that," he said.

"Well, you weren't telling me anything."

"Because I'm no one," he said.

"You keep saying that, but Caroline found you in Ireland and brought you back here for something."

"I have skills—"

"Eden called you a junkyard dog."

His head snapped back at that as if the words

hit a nerve. "She would know, I guess."

"Is that what you are?"

"No," he said. "It's what I was. Caroline found me and gave me a chance to be something else. I took it. That's all, Poppy. That's the story of me."

"Who put you in the hospital when you were young?"

He stood up from the chair in one fluid rush. Stalked me across the room, and I scuttled like a crab along the wall heading for that French door.

MY HEARTBEAT POUNDED in my ears, and I was aware that this man had a line and with that question it was probably somewhere behind me.

He smacked his hand against the wall beside my head, and I flinched at the sound. Expecting it to be my face that he hit. I slowly opened my eyes to find him watching me. So unreadable. A million miles deep.

"How bad do you want to know?" he asked. He stepped up against me, the hand I'd held out was useless against him. He pushed it back against me with his chest. His skin was hot under his fine shirt.

"I . . . don't," I said. My bravery gone. I was a paper doll. Crumpled when pressed.

"Oh, what a liar you are."

"Okay, you wanted to scare me? You wanted to warn me? Great. You did it. I'll stay away from Eden Morelli." I thought briefly of that favor I owed her, but I wasn't going to tell him about that. Or Jacob.

I wasn't going to tell him anything, anymore. I pushed against him, but he didn't budge. It was just the heat of his body. Against my hand. Against me. The longer he stayed there, unmoving, his heart beating against my hand, I started to wonder if this was a different game.

I looked up at him, the memories of his body pushing mine against that door, an unwelcome heat in my brain. In my body.

The hand I had pressed against his chest, shifted. Stroked. Over the firm curve of his chest, I brushed the bead of his nipple with my pinky, and his body trembled. *Trembled.* I did it again. Harder. I used just a little, the edge of my nail, and he licked his lip.

Fuck. What was I doing? And now that I was doing it how was I going to stop?

"Ask me," he said.

"Anything I want?"

He nodded. "But it will cost you."

"I don't have anything," I breathed. I was

pressing my sharp fingernails against his chest now. All of them, sinking deeper waiting for him to flinch or to stop me, but all he did was bite his lower lip and make dark noises in the back of his throat.

"You have more than you think," he said, and then suddenly he stepped away, leaving cold blank space behind him. He sat in the chair, his legs spread in a beam of moonlight. The rest of his body in shadow. "Ask me."

"Who hurt you when you were young?"

"My father," he said. "And then the priests. Take off your clothes."

My brain could not catch up. And I stood there, shaking with desire and worry. "Take off your clothes, Poppy. And I'll let you ask me another question."

"And if I don't?"

"I'll take them off for you."

I pulled the sweatshirt over my head. Unbuttoned my jeans and pushed them down. I stepped out of them, wearing a thin cotton camisole and a pair of high-cut panties. Hardly seductive.

You're not much to look at, are you?

But Ronan seemed to like to look.

His hands ran down his powerful thighs to his knees and then back up. Again, and then again.

And I realized what he wanted was to touch his cock and he was stopping himself. Well, I thought. That was interesting. It was too bad I didn't know what to do with the information. I was no Eden Morelli. I was just me.

"Ask," he said.

"Why are you doing this? With me?"

"Because you make it so easy."

He was hurting me, because I allowed him to. Because I *wanted* it.

Oh, I thought, suddenly cold in front of him. Embarrassed. Right.

I crossed my arms over my chest and crouched, reaching for my clothes. I knew better than to want what I could not have.

"And because the night we met I'd never seen anyone so beautiful," he said. In the stillness that followed his words, I wavered. I wavered because I wanted so badly to believe him. Despite all the proof.

"Don't lie." My voice cracked.

"Ask me."

"Are you lying?"

"I'm not. Now stand up straight." I didn't, still crouched. Still hiding. I wasn't this brave. "You made a deal with me. You could ask questions, but they would cost you."

"It costs too much," I said. "You . . . cost too much."

"Stand up, Princess. You have more questions. You risked your life going to Eden Morelli to find answers."

"She wouldn't hurt me."

"Don't be a fool, Poppy. She would snap your neck if it served her. Now ask me what you want to know."

I closed my eyes and found through some kind of magic, my back bone. Rising from the floor, I stood up straight again.

"What do you do for Caroline?"

"I fix problems," he said.

"What kinds of problems?"

"The kinds lawyers and accountants can't fix. That's two questions."

"What do you want?"

"Oh, Princess," he groaned, the tone of his voice changed, revealing in the low gravel, what this game cost him. "What *don't* I want from you?"

The force holding me to the wall was suddenly gone, and I stepped forward, desperate to touch him. Desperate to have him touch me.

"No," he said, and I froze. "Back against the wall."

"Don't you want me to . . . touch you?"

"No, Princess, I don't want you to touch me."

"Ron—"

"I want you to touch yourself."

I thought *what?* But the words didn't get past my lips.

"Princess," he said softly, like I was something sweet to him, and it pushed me into action. Back against the wall where he wanted me. I feared, no, total honesty—I knew. I knew that if he talked to me with that sweet voice, I'd do whatever he wanted. "Spread your legs."

I did, shy and spellbound.

He leaned forward into the moonlight. "Wider."

I stepped out wider. My underwear pulling to the side. "Do what you do when you're alone," he said.

"I don't." I licked my dry lips with a dryer tongue. Every bit of moisture in my body was between my legs. "I don't do anything when I'm alone. Not for a very long time."

His eyebrow lifted. "Why?"

"Because that part of me was beaten into submission," I told him starkly.

"Well, let's bring it back." He sat back into the shadows, and a cloud travelled over the moon outside the window and the room was suddenly dark. "You have beautiful breasts," he said. "Touch them for me."

The compliment and the darkness worked in his favor, and my hands came up to cup my breasts. My fingers finding my nipples hard beneath the thin camisole. My breasts ached to be touched.

With his voice telling me what to do, the electrical currents beneath my warm and soft skin hummed to life, and I sucked in a breath.

"You liked when I pulled your nipples. When I made them sting and burn."

I did. Yes. I remembered that. And I did it to myself. Between my legs I was hot. And suddenly achingly empty.

"Ronan," I whispered.

"Put a hand between your legs, Poppy."

I gasped when I did it. My own fingers felt so good.

"Are you wet?"

"Yes."

"How wet?"

"Very . . . wet."

I should be embarrassed. How was I not embarrassed?

The cloud slipped past the moon and the

room was suddenly illuminated. Brighter for those few moments of darkness.

"Show me," he said. I slipped my fingers out to show him. No idea if he could see it or not, but it hardly seemed to matter. Nothing really seemed to matter except his voice and the ache in my body. I closed my eyes and put my fingers back between my legs.

"No," he said. "Put your fingers in your mouth."

I blinked open my eyes, stunned at the suggestion.

"God, look at you. Still so fucking innocent after all this time. Put your fingers in your mouth. Taste yourself."

I opened my lips, slipped my fingers inside. I was salty. Musky. Like nothing I'd ever tasted before.

"Enough," he groaned, like he couldn't take anymore. "Pet yourself, Poppy."

Breathing hard, I slipped my wet fingers down my body, back between my legs.

"Remember the first time you did this?" he asked. "A girl alone in her bed?"

I nodded.

"How old were you?"

"Fifteen."

"What turned you on so hard you had to touch yourself?"

"Zilla's tennis coach."

"Tell me."

"He was nineteen. Mom hired him, probably to fuck him when Dad wasn't looking. He . . ." I brushed my clit, and power and lust surged through my body. I went back again. Again. Using my fingers against myself. "He . . . watched me."

"Did he touch you?"

"No. Never."

"Did you want him to?"

I shook my head.

"Tell me."

"No," I answered. "But I liked that he wanted to."

"I want to touch you," he said. I wanted him to touch me, too. So badly. My knees buckled, and I pushed my head back against the wall. My hips bowing.

"Why don't you?"

"Isn't this more fun?"

"I don't like games."

"That's because you've been playing them with the wrong person."

Enough. I thought. Enough of him and his

games. I closed my eyes, blocking him out.

"Poppy—"

"Shut up."

His chuckle was dark. Ominous. I waited for him to punish me, to tell me to stop. To say something mean.

"Do it, Poppy. Make yourself come."

My body was awake under my fingers. My body was my own under my fingers. And I remembered what I liked. How I liked to be touched. I remembered what I'd pushed away and forgotten about for so long. I came rushing back to myself. To my skin. My fingers. The ridge of my clit. The tender, wet opening of my body.

That summer of Zilla's tennis coach, I'd done this relentlessly. Finding every reason to go to my room so I could touch myself. When I started dating I was sure the boys in high school would figure out how to make me feel as good when they touched me as I was able to make myself feel when I was alone, but they just didn't have the attention span.

In college, Damon in my work/study program, he had the attention span and applied it to my clitoris in the dusty back rooms of the Linderman Library. He'd been sweet and studious and for a very nice month before my world came crashing down, I'd been infatuated with what he did to me and what he asked me to do to him.

It was a fine education in that library.

"What are you thinking of?" Ronan asked.

"The kid who used to finger-fuck me in the back room of the library."

"What else did he do to you?"

I was distracted by the pinch of my fingers. "Poppy? Did you let him fuck you?"

"No."

"Why not?"

Such a good question. "I just . . . didn't."

"Did you suck his dick?"

I nodded my head. Once.

"Did you like it?"

Oh god. His voice and the memory and my fingers . . . I was going to come. I bit my lower lip, my fingers working faster over my clit.

"Answer me."

"Yes."

"Did he put his mouth on you?"

"No."

"Why not?"

"I didn't . . ."

"Poppy."

"I didn't want him to," I blurted. It had seemed like a step too far for a back room at the

M. O'KEEFE

library. I'd have to take off my pants, and what if it didn't work? Or I didn't like it? I liked it when he put his hands in my underwear and sucked on my neck. I didn't need more.

"Did the senator?"

My bitter laugh caught on a gasp.

"Has anyone put their mouth on you?"

"No . . . oh god. Ronan—"

The orgasm that exploded between my legs made me cry out. Made my legs buckle. "Fuck," I said, teasing it out for as long as it would last. The major explosion faded, and lightning trails rippled through me. I braced myself against the bedside table and opened my eyes.

Only to find him right in front of me. A breath away. His eyes glittering. I jerked back like there was any distance to find between us, but the wall was at my back.

"Can I touch you?" he asked, and there was no game in his voice. No purr. No trick. There was only need. And it was what I liked about the tennis coach. Being needed. Like this. Dripping wet and soft.

And that he asked . . . that was different. I felt flush with some new power he'd never given me before.

"Yes."

What I expected; his fingers on my skin. His hand between my legs. My breasts grabbed in rough, desperate hands, none of it happened. This man . . . this dangerous mysterious man with all his secrets, went down on his knees in front of my body. His hands slid around my waist, pressing me against the wall. The heat of his hand, the shock of his touch made me gasp. My muscles shook.

"Spread your legs," he said, and I did it. Knowing exactly how wide he wanted, I gave it to him. That unfettered look between my legs. My soaking-wet panties. My slick thighs. My pink skin, usually hidden, completely revealed to him like this.

"No one has kissed this beautiful spot on your body?"

Speechless, I shook my head.

Without another word, he put his open mouth to me, breathing me in through the cotton. His tongue pressed against me, and I pushed up on my tiptoes, still sensitive from my orgasm. But that was why he had his hands on my waist. To keep me where he wanted me.

"Move your panties," he said against me.

"Ronan." I was raw. Shaking. There would be no other orgasm.

"Move them, Poppy."

And I did. I pushed my underwear aside, and he put his mouth back on me. Against me. He sucked me into his mouth. He tongued me and slipped his hands up to cup my breasts. What did I know about what my body could do? Nothing, apparently.

Because the next orgasm was picking me up in its fist, and I screamed, clutching his head, grinding myself against him. It was like some kind of door had been kicked open, and there was something new for me. Something I never expected.

Being touched like this was a revelation. Like suddenly being worshiped, when all my life I'd only been forsaken.

"Sorry," I breathed and let go of his head. He chuckled against my skin, licking my slick thighs like he wanted to taste everything. He pulled my underwear back over my body, covering me like it mattered at all. He kissed my belly. And then stood up.

His cock brushed against my belly, and I arched toward him, pressing myself against him. But his hands returned to my waist and pushed me back against the wall. His bent head rested against mine.

So long he stood there. Just breathing.

I reached for his face, but at the brush of my fingers he stepped away. The moment over.

"What else did you tell Eden Morelli?"

Blinking, I only gaped at him. My pleasure-soaked brain unable to catch up to what he was saying.

"Poppy!" he snapped, the sharp disapproval in his tone went to work on my instincts, and I reached down and grabbed my sweatshirt. Putting it over my shaking and sweaty body. "What else did you tell her?"

"I didn't . . . nothing. Nothing important."

"You are not the judge of what's important."

"Ronan, can we—" I stepped off the wall, and he stepped back. A reversal of our positions just a few minutes ago. "We talked about you. I asked how Caroline would have met you."

"And what did she say?"

"That Caroline was in the UK for oil drilling."

He pushed his hair back on his head, and it fell forward over his eyes. "Did you tell her anything about you?"

"No."

"Good. Keep—"

"Actually . . ."

"Fuck."

"She said the senator always seemed like a good guy and I . . . might have implied that he wasn't."

He nodded, his hair brushing the side of his face. "How much did you pay her?"

I licked my lips, searching for some kind of plausible lie.

"Poppy?"

"My sister paid her," I said. "That's . . . how I got in touch with Eden. My sister knows her."

I waited to see if he would buy my lie, and after a long minute he nodded. "All right. Can you promise me you won't be seeing Eden Morelli again?"

"Are you really trying to keep me safe?" I asked.

"Well." He was going to make a joke; I could hear it in his tone. "You don't make it easy—"

"Ronan."

He sighed and stepped back towards me like he was a magnet. My entire body was metal shavings I was drawn so hard to him.

"Why do you stay here?" he asked, brushing a damp hair off my forehead.

"In New York?"

"This house. Don't you have any place else to

go?"

I thought of the condo in Cabo. The house in the south of France. I'd never been to either of them, but I knew about them.

"This is my home," I said. Like he would care that I'd done all these renovations. That I'd built a shower and helped tile the kitchen. That I'd put some blood and sweat and more tears than I'd ever thought possible into this place and didn't that somehow make it mine?

My home had always been in Bishop's Landing. I didn't know a life off this hilltop.

"It's a shit home," he said.

"How would you know?" I asked. I didn't know if I was brave or stupid. "Have you ever had a home?"

His eyes glittered, and his silence wasn't an answer. This game we'd played tonight left me with a thousand more questions about him, while I kept stripping off pieces of myself to hand him.

"I just want a home," I whispered, sounding pathetic to my own ears.

"Homes are for old women. You should go," he said. "Take your sister and sit on a beach in Mexico or wherever girls like you sit on beaches."

"Girls like me?"

"You should drink and fuck tennis coaches

and sit around fulfilling your useless—"

"Why are you being cruel?"

"Because I am cruel," he said, leaning forward right into my space. His lips parted revealing his teeth like he wanted to bite me, and my stupid traitor body liked the idea. "I'm cruel, and you're a stupid spoiled princess, and you're in so far over your head you don't even realize you're drowning."

"But you're trying to save me?"

"You get in touch with the Morellis again, and you are on your own."

He left, and I stayed in the bedroom until I heard the beep of the alarm as he walked out one of the doors on the main floor. And then I ran down the steps and reset the alarm.

But it wasn't until I was in bed, freshly showered, and fully dressed, that I wondered how he got in my house in the first place.

CHAPTER TWELVE

"ARE YOU SURE you don't want to learn how to drive in a different car?" Theo asked as he got out of the town car parked at my front door. The day was bright and smelled like sunshine and spring. Which, not to sound super corny, meant that the day smelled like a fresh start.

I wore an old cashmere sweater that had a moth hole in it, but I'd kept because the color was this beautiful coral that I'd never seen anywhere else, and it made me happy to look at. I tossed a red scarf around my neck and pulled on thin leather gloves that I found in my drawer.

On my feet were my new standbys, my Converse tennis shoes. Looking at myself in the mirror this morning I was well aware that I hadn't dressed for myself in two long years, and the senator, should he see me in this, would demand I change.

Perhaps this outfit was ridiculous, but it felt

good on my body. And that was so novel and strange and . . . important.

"Do I have a different car?" I asked. I'd only ever seen the shiny black town car.

"The senator has a Porsche 911 and a corvette stingray. Or had . . . I guess. They're yours now."

Mine now. Wild. *What else did I own*, I wondered, *that I didn't even know about?*

But Porsches and Corvette Stingrays felt like advanced cars, and I was very much a beginner.

"No," I shook my head. "The town car sounds fine."

"All right," Theo said and walked around the car to the passenger seat.

I slid into the expensive leather driver seat and put my hands on the wheel.

"This is fun, isn't it?" I said.

"Yes, ma'am," Theo answered, and I caught his smile before he could put it back behind the mask he usually wore.

The sun was just coming up, and the spring mornings were cool, damp. All the green trees and grass were shrouded in a thin layer of mist. The Constantine Compound was over the hill in front of me. The turret just visible.

Why didn't I leave Bishop's Landing? I wondered. I'd spent most of the night thinking about

Ronan's words. There was nothing really keeping me here. Caroline. The executive director job, which I was pretty sure was just going to be for show.

I had more money than I knew what to do with. I had houses in other cities that I'd never been to.

I'd lived on this hill in Bishop's Landing for almost my entire life. Except for the year and a bit that I was at school, I'd lived in a house on this hill. I hadn't really ever vacationed anywhere. No girls' trips to Paris. No all-inclusives in Mexico. Perhaps the answer to why didn't I leave was I didn't know where to go?

Lord. That was sad, even for me.

But what I really felt was something so much more complicated. Something about my sister and my mother and the willow tree and how I'd never felt safe . . . anywhere.

"Ma'am?" Theo said.

"Call me Poppy."

"That's not . . ." I glanced over, and Theo was shaking his head. His blond hair was long with a curl to it, and it was a little wild in the damp morning. "No."

"Okay, but I'm going to call you Theo."

"That's fine."

"So, I'm going to call you by your name, and you're going to call me ma'am like we're on *Downton Abby* or something?"

"I don't know that show."

"We're the same age, Theo."

"No, ma'am, we're not." He was probably ten years older than me, which meant he was still young. We were both young. And now we were alone in the front seat of this car. As far as intimacy with a man, this would have ranked pretty high if Ronan hadn't come along and blown the curve by putting his mouth on me.

"Can I pay you to call me Poppy?" I asked.

He laughed and then tried to cover it up with a stern sounding cough. "You are very—" he stopped himself. Shook his head.

"I'm what?"

"Different. This morning." Oh, how helplessly he said that. Like he wished it wasn't true. Or that he wished he didn't notice. But he wasn't wrong—I *was* different. And it was time for my life to look a little different, too.

"You know something," I said, opening the driver side door to get out. "I would like to drive the Porsche."

Theo's eyes went wide and his smile—if you could call it that—was very nearly approving. "It's a stick shift," he said.

"That's fine," I said, though it probably wasn't.

Ten minutes later I was grinding my way down the hill from my house.

"Clutch," he said. Again.

"Right, right." There was a small hill and a stop sign ahead. "Oh no. Should we go back and get the town car?"

"Don't be scared," he said. "And you're doing fine. No one is great at driving a stick shift right away."

"You're lying."

"I'm not, ma'am."

"I'm going to stall it."

"Clutch, shift, gas. You can do it."

Seamlessly, I shifted out of first into second. No stalling. No grinding.

I gasped with delight.

"Nice," he said.

Instantly I did something that made the car shudder and grind. "Oh my god, this is awful. Is it me? Is it this car?"

"It's the stick shift and you're doing great. You really are." Theo was a very enthusiastic teacher and surprisingly calming. "On this hill, careful you don't . . ."

The car stalled.

"Do that?" I asked.

Theo actually laughed, which cut my nervous energy in two, and then I was laughing.

I put the car in park and restarted it just as a man in black training pants and a sweat-stained shirt ran across the road in front of us. At the sound of the car starting, he glanced over, and our eyes met.

"Ronan," I breathed.

He stopped in the middle of the road, facing us. His unreadable eyes traveling from Theo's face to mine.

His dark hair was slick on his forehead, and his chest was heaving. In the thin running gear, he seemed bigger than he usually did. His chest was wide. His shoulders broad. Less a deadly blade and more a blunt object.

He grabbed the hem of his shirt and used it to wipe his face, revealing the pale skin of his stomach. The ripple of muscle.

My smile faded slowly from my face as my body remembered what he did to it last night. My body wanted more. So much more. All at once my body wanted everything this man could do to it.

"Come on, man," Theo said and reached over

and honked the horn. The car was tiny, and Theo was not a small man. We were shoulder to shoulder in the front seat, and when he reached past me we touched even more.

Ronan saw it all. But his face registered nothing. Nothing at all.

What is he thinking? Did he care? Did it matter that I was sitting so close to another man? I smiled to see if there was a reaction. His face didn't even reveal that he knew me. Let alone that he'd put his mouth on me.

He walked to the side of the road and watched us as we drove by. The gears grinding, the car lurching.

I looked back in the rear-view mirror, and he was still there. Still watching.

"You all right, Poppy?" Theo asked. Dropping the ma'am, and I quite suddenly wanted it back. The distance. Which was ridiculous. Ronan wasn't my . . . anything. His dark stare, that I still felt on the back of my neck, was another one of his games.

"I'm fine," I said, and I pushed the clutch, shifted to third and took off down the hill.

Monday morning Theo drove me into the city.

"You sure you don't want to try?" he asked.

The window was rolled down, and his eyes met mine in the rear-view mirror. They were nice eyes. Brown and big. Kinder than I'd ever noticed.

"Driving around Bishop's Landing is one thing. Manhattan is another thing all together. I'm just trying to save your life, Theo."

"Well, I appreciate that, Poppy."

My name in his mouth sent a strange ripple through me. I wasn't sure if I was uncomfortable or if I liked it.

My phone rang, saving me from contemplating kissing Theo in order to forget Ronan and what a mess that would be. The screen said Zilla.

"Excuse me," I said to Theo.

"Of course," Theo said and pushed the button that made the window between us slide up.

"Hey," I said. "How are you, Zilla?"

"I'm fine. Good. How are you? I didn't hear from you after your meeting with Eden."

"Oh, right," I said, that weird meeting forgotten after Ronan and then the driving lesson. "It was fine. I mean. I didn't get a lot of information. It was probably a mistake trying to pry."

There was a second of silence on Zilla's side. "You're joking, right?"

"No. I mean. I appreciate your effort but—"

"My effort?" She laughed. "God you're such

an infant sometimes, Poppy."

That stung. Really stung. But it also worried me. "Are you all right?" I asked.

"Oh Jesus Christ," she said. "For once this isn't about my mistakes. You owe Eden Morelli a favor, Poppy."

"I know."

"Do you know what kind of favors she wants?"

"No."

"Bloody ones. Criminal ones."

"Zilla—"

"And you don't have the senator there to protect you."

"Protect me!" I scoffed, the sound scraping through my throat. "Is that what you thought he did?"

"No," my sister said, reeling herself in. "Of course not. I'm just saying the Constantine/Morelli world works differently."

"I know how the world works," I snapped. "The world kills your mother when you're sixteen and gives you a father who burns through all the money. The world gives your sister a psychotic break—"

"Poppy," she breathed.

"And takes away every choice we have except

one. One choice. One choice who broke my finger because he could. Who threw books at my head. Who left bruises on my body. Who was so driven to have a baby that my feelings on the matter did not count."

I closed my eyes and pressed my shaking fingers to my eyes. "Don't tell me how the world works," I whispered. "I'll talk to you later."

Without giving her a chance to say anything, I hung up. And because I knew she would call back with all her apologies, I turned off my phone.

The Halcyon Building was a skyscraper in midtown. Walking up to it I always felt like a character in *Legally Blonde*. A little out of place but determined to try. There was a jazzy little number playing in the background, something plucky. Today I felt that so keenly it was like a laugh or a sob caught in my throat. I was going to do this. Executive director of a million-dollar foundation. If I had doubts, I was trying hard to squash them under some undeserved optimism. Unearned confidence.

But Caroline was right. I had ideas. Good ones. And now I had a lot of money to put them into action.

I was new at believing in myself so it took a second, but by the time I got in the front door I was swinging my new briefcase around like I was about to burst into song. The foundation was on the 24th floor, and when the elevator doors opened there was a big wide desk with 'Better Families, Better New York' in gold and black lettering against a white wall.

Justin was sitting there and looked stunned to see me. And I was a little stunned to see him.

"Poppy?" he said, getting to his feet. "I didn't know you were coming in today?"

"I told Caroline I'd be coming in today."

"Oh no," he said. "My mistake. Let me call her, and she can be here in twenty minutes."

"Actually." I leaned forward, speaking conspiratorially. "I don't want a big fuss, and we both know that Caroline is the definition of a big fuss."

Justin smiled, and I smiled back at him, relieved that he wasn't offended by the joke. But also suddenly wondering if he was going to go and tell Caroline. But then that thought was disloyal, so I shoved the whole thing aside.

"Seriously. I just want to look around. But what are you doing here?"

"Caroline wanted me to come down to set up some systems."

"Oh. Well, systems are good." *What kind of systems did people have to set up?* I wondered.

"The phones are working. Interoffice email. The official receptionist starts next week."

Oh. Those systems.

He began to pull documents off the desk and hand them to me. "Here's a list of applicants for the position of your assistant. We can call them for interviews whenever you're ready." There was another stack of papers. "Here are the first rounds of funding requests. I haven't vetted any of them." He handed me another stack. "And here is the old funding criteria from Caroline's other founda-tions. We thought that might be a good jumping-off place." More stacks of paper. More and more and more. "Here are media requests. Again. I haven't vetted all of them. But if you're ready to start, flag the ones you like, and Caroline will look over them."

"Sure," I said, overwhelmed and trying not to be. "Where's my . . . desk?"

He smiled at me, and I had to admit I did like Justin. He was competent and kind. It wasn't his fault that he always looked like a little puppy.

"Follow me. I think you will be very pleased."

We rounded the desk into a small open con-cept room with two desks. One of them positioned in front of another closed door. Justin opened it and stepped back, smiling.

"Oh my gosh," I whispered, stepping into the office. One whole wall was nothing but windows, floor to ceiling. A beautiful cherry wood Queen Anne desk with a sleek computer monitor on top. The wall opposite the windows had a massive white board and calendar. Three chairs set up with small tables between them. Morning meetings with my team. It was feminine and majestic and so, so amazing.

"Caroline thought you might enjoy this set up. She thought you'd want to be a part of things, instead of just making decisions in your office."

"It's amazing," I said.

Justin looked down at his watch. "I have to go," he said.

"Of course."

"I will email you the codes to lock up. Passwords for the computers. And other than that . . ." He smiled at me. "Feel free to poke around all you like."

Justin left, and I heard the beep of the main door and figured he must have engaged the alarm, and so all alone and feeling very safe and very excited, I sat down behind my desk and got to work.

I wasn't sure what time it was when the door beeped again. The sun was setting over the west side of the city, and I was starving. "Hello?" I said. "Justin is that—"

Into my new world; my beautiful feminine space where I was hoping to build my team and my future, walked Ronan Byrne. In a dark suit and a darker expression.

"What are you doing here?" I asked and got to my feet. No matter how our encounters ended, they started with me being scared of him, and I wasn't sure if that was stupid, or smart. But no matter what he did to my body—my brain did not trust him.

The thing about this man, the awful terrible thing about him was what he made me feel. The sight of him in my doorway triggered my fight or flight instinct, and he also turned me on. My belly was soft for him. And I didn't understand how he managed to do all of that, or what I was supposed to do with the push and pull of it all. It was too much.

He was too much.

"I'm just looking around." He put his hands in his pockets, like he was some regular guy doing some regular thing. "Quite a set up."

He stepped forward, and I stepped sideways thinking if I had to, I might be able to get to the door. Immediately he lifted his hands.

"I'm not here to touch you," he said, his lips kicked up with that charming half-smile my body loved so much. "I swear it."

I didn't believe him. Not a bit.

"How'd you know I was here?"

"Caroline told me to come check on you."

"You always do what Caroline tells you?" The words came out snappy and sharp. A red flag in front of a bull, and as soon as they were out of my mouth I regretted them.

His eyes seared me. My skin by all rights should have been blackened and smoky. I stepped back, waiting for him to come across this room, put his hand around my neck and pin me to the wall.

Just thinking it I was scared. And wet between my legs.

What is wrong with me?

"Have you eaten?" he asked. I blinked at the change of subject.

"No," I said. "But how—"

"Let's go get something," he said, jerking his head to the door.

I blinked at him, shook, absolutely shook by this strange version of him. "What's wrong with you?"

"I offered to feed you, and you think something's wrong?"

"Yeah."

"You'd rather I put my hand down your pants?" He nodded at my body. I'd taken off the jacket and just wore a cream shell and my black pants.

"No." *Yes.*

"I could order something up," he said. "A salad—"

"What the fuck are you doing?" I snapped.

"What the fuck are you doing?" he snapped back, his eyes alight, and the half step he took towards me lit me up like a bonfire. But then he stopped. Reined himself back in. "Justin said you'd been here since ten. It's four now." He looked around. "And I don't think you've eaten anything."

I wasn't hungry. But now my stomach growled. *Now* I was ravenous.

With his phone out, he turned, facing the window and the four o'clock sun that came in like butter to the room. A quick call and lunch was coming.

And I saw how this might spin out. We might sit down, he might have a sandwich. I might have a salad. He'd revert to the charming man he'd been at that party. I might revert to not being terrified and turned on at the same time. All of that might happen. But what I couldn't understand was why?

I put my hands on my hips and didn't sit down. "What are you after, Ronan?"

"Well, Poppy." He ran a hand through his hair. The dark strands holding themselves in place for just a second before slipping down over his eyes. "I believe I owe you an apology."

That was not at all what I was expecting, and I actually took a step back.

"I've shocked you. Well, frankly, the way I've treated you, I've shocked myself. I think . . ." He glanced around. "Is there a drink in here somewhere?"

"Water?"

"A proper drink, like."

In the credenza behind my desk there was a pretty stocked bar. Justin thought of everything. "What would you like?"

"Is Jameson's too much to ask for?" he asked.

I opened the cabinet and checked inside. "Apparently not. Though . . . there's no ice or anything."

"That's fine. Will you join me?"

Who the fuck was this guy? "In straight whiskey? No." I pulled out a bottle of fizzy water. The last time I had a drink in front of this guy things went off the rails real fast. Of course, they went off the rails the second time when I was sober-ish. Nope. I was going to keep my wits about me.

"I swear to you, Poppy. I will not touch you," he said, like he could read my mind.

But, I thought, *did I want him to touch me?*

"Here," I said and handed him the bottle and the glass from the credenza, and I sat down in my chair and twisted off the top of the water.

"So," I said. "You were about to explain why you've been such an asshole."

"Well." He sat with his drink in the chair across from my desk. He looked so dark in this bright room. But oddly right, like he gave this space contrast and balance. "Let's not get confused. Part of me being an asshole, you liked well enough."

Was this . . . was he teasing me? All his danger was turned down to some flirty comradery. Like we were at a reunion, "*remember when I called you pathetic and made you come so hard your brain broke? Good times.*"

Except I wasn't going to give him that. I wasn't going to give him anything.

"I don't like anything about you, Ronan."

"Well, it's easier to surrender when you can

hate the person forcing you to do it," he said, looking out the windows at the city.

"There is not one situation I can imagine where you give up control," I said.

"I don't know," he said, his eyes still on the clouds, birds making their way across town. "The priests were fond of my surrender."

Oh. Right. Now I felt foolish. "I'm sorry," I felt compelled to say.

"Being hurt by people who were supposed to care for us is something we have in common," he said. When he finally turned to look at me, I was startled to be caught staring at him.

"You're talking about my husband?" I said. "I don't know if he was ever supposed to care for me."

"Millennia of married people would say otherwise."

"I think a millennia of married people probably prove my point."

"My god, Poppy, are you trying to convince me that you're jaded?"

"Are you trying to convince me you're a romantic?"

"No chance of that," he said with a laugh and another sip of his whiskey. "You were so young when I met you at that party. And when I found out who you were and what—" he licked his lips, and my stomach coiled with some intense emotion, "—was happening to you. I was angry, and there was nothing I could do about it. So, it was easier to be angry with you."

I opened my mouth. Shut it. No one had been so honest with me in years. Not even my sister. Not even Caroline.

"That's awful," I said for the lack of anything better to say.

"I know."

There was a knock at the door and a stranger's voice saying "hello."

"Food," Ronan said. He set his whiskey down and went to go answer the delivery guy, while I sat there reeling. *Was this true?* I wondered. Was this version of him real? Why would he lie? Why would he feign kindness? Or vulnerability?

All those questions did was convince me further that I should leave. Grab my coat. Lock up and let him have his dinner alone. I was at the very start of something exciting in this office, and he'd already changed the whole dynamic of the place with his honesty and his dark good looks.

If I wanted something to be mine, then I had to make it. I had to make choices. Hard ones. I put my coat on. Put the bottle of whiskey back in the credenza. Shoved files into my briefcase. I'd call Theo and tell him to pull—

Ronan came back into the room carrying two plastic bags, surrounded by the most delicious smells of garlic and fresh herbs. Butter. My stomach growled. My resolve weakened.

"You're leaving?" he said.

"I think it's best," I said.

"It's just food," he said, and I realized my face must register my distrust. "It's here and you're hungry. I'll leave."

"That's the nicest thing you've said to me," I told him.

"That's not true. But I will leave you to eat in peace." He set the bags down on the edge of the desk, and the smells were even more delicious.

"What is it?" I asked.

"Spanish food. From a place down the corner."

"You like Spanish food?"

"There are a lot of things about me you don't know," he said.

Oh, for fuck's sake. How dramatic could I be.

"Sit," I said. "You're hungry, too."

His smile was a flash, and in that flash I saw what he must have been like when he was younger. When there was something grateful and happy left in him. "I'm not going to lie," he said. "I'm starving."

He started to take out the boxes, opening them to reveal paella with juicy black-shelled mussels, grilled octopus, flaky manchego cheese, and roasted red peppers. Pale almonds and bright green olives. He set out napkins and plastic utensils. There were bottles of water. And what looked like a to-go cup of coffee.

"Here," he said, handing me a paper plate while I stood there staring at the feast he made happen. For me. I mean, for us, sure. But . . . for me. "What's wrong? You don't like Spanish?"

"No," I said. "I love it." My mouth was actually watering. "I'm just grateful. Thank you."

Again, that half smile from him. That sparkle in the corner of his eye, the way he ducked his head as he scooped up the rice and seafood covered in aioli and fresh bright green herbs.

I sat down and took some cheese, olives, and bread.

"So, you're going to be the executive director of the foundation," he said, sitting back with octopus and a mound of saffron yellow rice, flecked with fresh green peas. "Are you excited?"

"Nervous."

"Why?"

"I'm not—" I almost said 'qualified' but I

wasn't going to reveal that to him. He already knew too much. "It's just been a while since I've worked."

"Did you always want to work with charities?"

"No." I laughed. "I wanted to teach fifth grade."

"A teacher!"

"Does it seem so ridiculous?"

"Not at all. Why fifth?"

"Because Mrs. Jordal was my fifth-grade teacher, and she was the best teacher ever. And I like the age. Not little kids, but not yet teenagers."

"So? Why aren't you a teacher?"

I thought back to the conversation I'd had with the senator.

"*I need you to be my wife. To travel with me. To manage functions and throw parties. You can't teach school and be the wife of a senator.*"

"*That's not true,*" I said. "*There are plenty of senator's wives who keep—*"

"*You can run the foundation, if you feel like being my wife isn't enough for you.*"

"*Jim,*" I said, putting my hand on the desk between us. "*That's not what I mean—*"

So fast, like a snake, Jim lifted the hard-backed book in front of him and smashed it down on my hand.

"Poppy?"

I blinked. Flexed the fingers of the hand he'd hurt. There'd been no broken bones, but I hadn't been able to hold anything in that hand for a week. And the bruise had been purple and green for even longer.

"Sorry," I said. "I got married." I shrugged like that explained everything. Like a shrug could encapsulate the slow shrinking of my world.

"And you stopped wanting to teach?"

I set down my fork, feeling heckled by his questions. "What about you? Did you always want to be a . . . whatever you are for rich people?"

He smiled and then laughed. "No. I wanted to be a priest." My mouth hung open. "When I was little and where I was from the priests had a lot of power. And if it was get hurt or hurt someone, I reckoned I'd rather not be hurt."

"It's hard to imagine you as a priest."

He took a bite of rice and shrugged. I ate yet another piece of cheese.

"How did you end up working for Caroline?"

I was watching so I saw it, the tiny freeze. The way he set down his fork and instead of feeding himself he wiped his mouth with a napkin. "She was in the UK, and I did some work for her there."

"Doing what?"

"Solving some problems with oil companies."

"Are you a lawyer?"

That made him laugh. "A negotiator."

I didn't exactly know what that meant, but I nodded like I did.

"For what it's worth," he said, sitting back in his chair, the plate he'd made for himself empty. "I think you'd be a great teacher."

"Why?" I laughed. "Nothing you know about me has anything to do with teaching." I blushed as I said it. He knew outrageous things about me.

"You're patient. And kind. Empathetic. Intelligent. You understand the value of small braveries." I set down my plate, my fingers suddenly shaking. "And you're beautiful. Which I think probably goes a long way with children."

I stood up because I didn't know what else to do. "I . . . ah . . . I have to go," I said.

"Because I called you beautiful?" he asked.

And smart and kind and the small braveries thing. All of it. I hadn't been paid a compliment in years, and that was too many.

Too much. Just like him.

Even if they were lies, they were the kindest lies someone had told me in so long.

"This was lovely, really," I said. I started shoving leftovers and dirty plates in bags. Cleaning up so I didn't have to look at him. "And I'm glad we can put all that other stuff behind us. And maybe be friends?" Though honestly, I couldn't imagine that. It would be like being friends with a wild animal. Something vicious and unpredictable. I'd done that already. I'd married a monster whose moods made me bleed.

"Stuff?" he said. "Friends? Are you talking in code?"

I saw him stand up out of the corner of my eye and abandoned the cleaning up to step back. Away.

"Poppy? What did I say?"

I forced myself to look at him. A small bravery. "What do you really want?" I asked, suddenly seeing through this all so well. So clearly. This was just another game. Kindness and dinner instead of cruelty and sex.

He took a breath and gave me a heartbreaker's smile. Devastating. "When I met Caroline," he said. "I was wild. Absolutely wild. I'd run from the school and was doing awful things, *awful* things for a gang in Belfast. And I tried to rob her. Not like a snatch and grab but, I tried to." He laughed, shaking his head. "It's so embarrassing.

But I tried to charm her. I sat next to her in a hotel bar, pretending to be some kind of nob. I bought her a martini, and I don't think I was old enough to drink. But, I got her purse and legged it. Got halfway down the block before one of her men grabbed me, dragged me back to her. She told me I was clever." His blue eyes pierced mine. "And I clearly wasn't, but I so badly wanted to be. I wanted to be clever and to belong in that hotel bar. I wanted to be anything but what I was. And her words watered a seed in me, and I decided right then and there that I'd be clever. For her."

"That's a real sweet story, Ronan, but what's your point?"

"I was clever. I had to be, to still be kicking, like. But I didn't believe it until she told me."

"You think I need you to tell me I'm smart so I'll believe it?" I scoffed and he shrugged.

"I think your husband told you awful lies about yourself and with no one around to tell you different, to remind you that you're smart and kind and all those other things you are, it was easy to believe him."

"Oh, this is rich coming from you." I didn't believe him. Because I couldn't. I couldn't risk it. I couldn't risk him or this dinner or his kindness. So, I struck out. "You're a fucking liar—"

And there he was, his body against mine pressing me to the credenza. He'd moved so fast, dropped the act *so fast* that I laughed breathlessly.

Yeah. There you are.

"Oh my god, your mouth," he whispered. "Your mouth makes me crazy. You're like a cat who keeps biting the hand that feeds you. And you don't seem to realize that you are soft and tiny and inconsequential." His hand came up to my face. His thumb against my lip, and I bared my teeth and snapped at him.

He laughed and grabbed my face in that hand, his fingers out of reach of my teeth.

"I could crush you, Poppy. Absolutely crush you, and I don't know if you don't realize it or if you just don't care."

"Fuck you."

I lifted my knee to hammer him in the crotch, but that too, he saw coming. And he kicked my feet out wide so I was unstable. He held me up by the grip on my face. The press of his hips against mine.

"Stop playing these fucking games and tell me what you want," I snapped.

"What I want is irrelevant," he said, almost kissing my lips. Again I tried to bite him, snarling this time. "Stop it and listen to me." He shook me like a rag doll. "I cannot say this more plain. You need to leave here."

"I'm trying, asshole. You're the one—"

"New York. Bishop's Landing, this goddamn foundation. You need to go far, far away."

"This is my home."

"Is it? Seems to me it's the place you've been used and hurt and lied to. You've been tricked and—"

"Shut up!"

"You know it's true, Poppy. You're gullible but you aren't stup—"

"Shut up!" I screamed. And my voice rang and echoed and pierced his expression. I was panting in his arms. Panting.

"I'm sorry," he whispered. "I'm so fucking sorry."

And he kissed me. He kissed me like his world was ending. And I was so stunned and scared that I stood there and I let him. I let him kiss me. Ravage me. His hand left my face, curled up into my hair, pulling until it hurt. "I'm sorry," he said again. Kissing and kissing and kissing me. "Poppy, don't make the mistakes I've made. Don't—"

There was a beep of the outer door opening, and Ronan left my body so fast I stumbled, catching myself against the desk.

"Poppy?" It was Theo.

This was some kind of total breach of driver etiquette. Never would he have come looking for Jim. Or me, previous to the driving lessons.

But never in my life had I been so glad to have destroyed protocols. I'd been weakening against Ronan's mouth. The bittersweet words he'd said. What mistakes had he made? What mistakes was he talking about? Staying when he should go?

"Back here!" I said and patted down my hair. Straightened my jacket. Without looking at me, Ronan grabbed the garbage from our meal.

"I'm sorry," Theo said as he came walking in, a big smile on his face. A smile that disappeared when he saw Ronan. And his face snapped back into that passive employee look that I'd been surrounded by during my marriage.

Ronan was doing the same.

It was like they were both in disguise.

"I got a notification from the alarm company a while ago," Theo said. "I thought you would have gotten it too, but when you didn't come down—"

"Alarm company?" I grabbed my phone from my purse. I'd turned it off after the fight with my sister and then forgotten to turn it back on as I worked.

There were four missed calls from the alarm company.

"What's happened?" Ronan asked, and Theo gave him a sharp look before looking at me. There was a beat of silence before I realized Theo wasn't going to say anything in front of Ronan unless I told him it was okay.

Ronan realized this too and stepped forward like he'd take Theo apart with one hand.

"It's fine," I said, holding up my hand like a traffic cop, not sure if it would stop Ronan. But it did. "You can tell me."

"No one has gone inside," he said. "But . . ." He pulled out his own phone and showed me the screen. There on my back deck was a roaring fire in the fire pit. A dark figure sitting in one of the chairs turned and faced the camera like she knew it was there. Cheekily, the figure waved.

Zilla.

"It's my sister," I said.

She drove to my house and sat outside by the fire because we fought.

"Let's go," I said.

"I'll go back downstairs," Theo said. "The car will be waiting."

"Thank you." And then proving how far I was

from kind, from sweet, I turned to Ronan. "Theo, this is Ronan. He works for Caroline."

Briefly, Ronan's eyes met mine, and if he had a reaction to this reestablishment of power, he showed nothing. "Nice to meet you," Ronan lied.

"Likewise." My guess was Theo was lying too. And he lingered, as if afraid to leave us alone together.

"I'll be right down," I said with a smile, easing his departure out the door. I felt undone. By the kiss. By the whole night. And I didn't know how to manage any of this.

Once Theo was gone, I gathered my things as Ronan waited by the door.

"Are you all right?" he asked, and the question brought me up short. His concern brought me up short.

"Fine."

"Your sister—"

"What about her?" I snapped.

"Is it a good thing she's at your house?"

It felt like he was truly concerned. Worried. And I didn't trust that for one moment. As much as I might want to. As much as it might be nice to lay down the load that was loving my sister at anyone's feet but my own.

Not his, I had to remind myself. Don't be so

stupid.

"It is," I said, which was true, but not the whole truth.

"Good."

He waited for me to gather my things and walk out the door, turning the lights off as I went. I set the alarm while he stood in the hallway waiting for me.

"You don't have to—"

"I know."

At the elevator we stood there, side by side. If I took a deep breath my shoulder would touch his, so I took a tiny step away.

"Poppy," he said, looking down at the garbage.

The elevator opened and I stepped in, expecting him to follow but he didn't. And there was something ominous about him on one side of the closing doors and me on the other. Something that made the hair on the back of my neck stand up. It was like the scene in those movies when the trap is closing around a character.

The door started to slide shut, and I slapped my hand against it.

I wondered if anything he'd said to me tonight was real.

Some, I thought. In the way of all liars, Ronan

had probably seeded his lies with small truths. The story about Caroline and the purse stealing, I could see that unfolding. The priests.

And I imagined so many mistakes in his past. More than mine, maybe.

But I didn't imagine him being sorry for a single one of them.

"What?" I asked, suddenly really afraid.

Ronan leaned in. "Don't trust anyone," he said. "Not that fucking driver. Not even your sister."

"And I'm supposed to trust you?" That was laughable. But also tragic. Because he'd set the bait so well, and I wanted to trust him.

"No," he said quietly. "Don't trust me, either."

I lifted my hand, stepped back against the wall of the elevator and watched his beautiful face until the doors shut and I was hurtling down to a life I didn't recognize. Couldn't trust.

And wasn't sure I even wanted.

CHAPTER THIRTEEN

T HE SUMMER I was twelve and Zilla was ten, the house changed. There were strange electric currents all originating from our mother. So Zilla and I spent the summer absolutely wild. The staff attempted to rein us in, make us bathe and feed us meals at the table, but Mom with a negligent wave of her hand, ordained our madness. We practically lived under the willow tree by the pond, returning to the house to get jars of peanut butter and cheese sticks from the fridge. Mom would go days without talking to us or seeing us, and then suddenly we'd be whisked up and taken to the city for dinners at fancy restaurants that had to accommodate us in our grubby summer clothes because of who Mom was. If she noticed how dirty we were, how red from days spent outdoors, our complexions an absolute explosion of freckles, she never said. She said nothing about how small all my clothes were. Or how self-conscious I was of the sudden puffiness of my nipples under my t-shirt.

We, however, noticed how Mom grew thinner and thinner. How she smoked non-stop and seemed to have conversations with people who weren't there.

Mom had turned off the central air and opened the windows, letting in all the heat and humidity, telling us we needed to actually feel the weather instead of living in zip lock bags. I didn't know what that meant, but it was really hot in our house. We only knew Dad was home because the air would be back on.

But, on what felt like the hottest day of that summer, after a night the cicadas had kept us up with their noise, I was lying listless and sweating in the living room when Zilla came running past me.

"Come on," she said and kept running. Through the living room, out the formal dining room, out the sliding doors through the sun room where Mom was sleeping in the shade.

I followed. Of course I followed. I chased my sister across the bright green lawn all the way down to the willow tree at the corner of the property right by the pond.

"What are you doing?" I asked, pushing aside the long snaky branches to find my sister Zilla with two cans of Coke she'd snuck out of the fridge. Mom drank the Coke with rum on nights when Dad was working, which that summer was every night. Sometimes Mom would let us have sips. But whole cans were reserved for special occasions that never seemed to come.

In the house where there were no rules, it was the only rule. The Coke was not for us.

"Oh my gosh, you stole them from the fridge."

"Stole? We live here too."

There was an argument to be made against Zilla. And usually I made them. But cold drops of condensation were gliding down the bright red cans, and I was so thirsty. And so tired. And, though I'd never say it out loud, so scared of what was happening in our house.

"No one is going to know," Zilla said, which really wasn't true, but for a second I decided to believe her. To let the future worry about itself.

We popped open the tops and drank down half the cans in big, long gulps.

The sugar and the cold and the thrill of it went right to my head. I stood up and kicked off my flip flops and peeled off my shorts.

"What are you doing?" Zilla asked.

"I'm going swimming."

"Naked?" Zilla cried like it was scandalous and amazing. And it was. I was. We went swimming plenty, but always in our swimsuits. Which hung in the tree we were standing under. It would take nothing to just pull them on. But I wasn't going to waste a precious minute pulling on last year's speedo that was too small and left bright red marks on my shoulders and thighs.

"Yep."

Naked as the day I was born, I pushed out from beneath the willow limbs that swept across the bright purple and white heads of the wild violets and went sprinting to the pond.

At the muddy edge of the black water, I paused. Courage deserting me. There were gardeners. And people around. Mom always said there were snakes in the pond, but that never seemed to bother me when I had my suit on. And then Zilla came sprinting past me into the water. Her naked body an arrow into the deep. She surfaced, hair streaming over her wildly happy face.

"Don't chicken out now!" she cried, and I raced in after her.

I could count on my hand the number of times I'd been brave. That was one of them. It was hard to remember if marrying the senator had been brave, I'd felt so scared. So desperate to make sure my sister was safe that I would have done anything.

As soon as I got out of the car in front of my house, I could smell the fire my sister had built in the back. And I won't lie, it gave me a pause. A quick second with my heart in my throat. Four years ago, we'd known Zilla was in trouble for a while, but when the fire happened after Dad died and the truth came out . . . it made her psychosis very real.

But that was four years ago, and she was better.

In the house, I kicked off my shoes, took off my jacket and grabbed my college sweatshirt I'd left in the kitchen. The benefit of no cleaning lady was that everything was exactly where I left it.

I opened the sliding doors to the back, and my sister turned in her seat.

"Finally," she said.

"What are you doing here?" I asked.

"I didn't like fighting with you."

"I don't like fighting with you either," I said.

"And since your husband isn't here to kick me out, I thought I'd come make amends in person." Zilla smiled at me, and I remembered that girl with the Coke cans beneath the willow tree with an ache so pure it took my breath away. "Are you mad?" Zilla asked in my silence.

"No." I practically ran across the deck to hug her. "I'm sorry we fought, too. And I'm so glad you're here. Are you cold?"

"No. This fire is kinda amazing, if I do say so myself," Zilla said. I felt the heat all along my side and realized she'd pushed the chairs back so she wouldn't roast. Don't say anything, I told myself. Every fire doesn't have to circle back to *that* fire.

"Are you hungry?"

"No. I'm fine. Just . . . sit with me."

I sat beside her in the cushioned love seat. We sat facing each other. Both of us with our legs tucked up, an arm stretched across the back of the cushions.

"Hey," I said, not wanting to think about my sister and fires. "Remember that summer we practically lived under the willow tree?"

"Of course. We were feral."

I laughed. "Do you remember the day with the Cokes?"

"And the skinny-dipping?" Zilla laughed, her face lit up by the fire. "I'll never forget your bare butt running out to that pond. I could not believe you were doing it."

"Me neither, frankly. I blame the pop."

"Whatever lets you sleep at night." Zilla laughed. "But I always thought you were a little more wild than you let on. You just needed a reason."

I thought of Ronan and the way he made me feel. Like I was touching a part of myself that I never knew existed. Like a lost moon.

"Dad was pissed," Zilla said.

"What are you talking about? Dad never found out."

Zilla looked at me, earnest and serious, clear and focused. "Of course he did, Poppy," she said almost like she pitied me. "The housekeeper told him everything we did that summer."

"What? Why didn't he say anything? Or do anything?"

"To stop Mom? To take care of us? I have no idea. But the skinny dipping got placed firmly on my shoulders, and I got spanked. For real."

I blinked, searching through my memory for some proof of this. But there was none. We swam. Went inside and ate turkey sandwiches. I finished reading *Twilight*. Zilla fell asleep in the recliner, snoring in the heat.

"That night," Zilla said. "When Dad came home. He called me into his office."

"But why didn't I get in trouble too?"

"Because I said it was only me. And he believed me."

"But it was both of us."

"Yeah, I know, dummy. I was protecting you. I know that seems inconceivable, but I've done things too, you know. To take care of you. To make sure you were okay."

The fierce edge in her voice made me sit up straight. "What are you talking about?"

"Oh don't look so scared, Poppy. Nothing dramatic. I'm just saying some things are worth the consequences."

I thought of Ronan and had to agree.

"Where have you been?" Zilla asked.

"In the city," I said with a sigh. "I'm taking the executive director position at the foundation."

Zilla's eyebrows hit her hairline.

"What?" I asked.

"Nothing. It's just . . . do you want to do that?"

"Why is that suddenly what everyone is asking me? No one has ever cared so much about what I do with my life."

"That's not true," Zilla said with her fierceness. "It's just been a while since you had a choice."

"Do you think I can't do it?"

"I think you can do whatever you want, but you've been making decisions based on the opinions of other people for a while now. You should get to decide for yourself."

How politely everyone said it. It was like we were all speaking code.

"It's nice to have something to do," I said. "To be useful."

"You could be useful in a million ways," Zilla said. "Not just in the ways she allows you to be."

"She being Caroline?"

Zilla shrugged.

What would it be like, I wondered, to live like Zilla. To not see or not care about all the strings that attached us to other people. All the ways our actions had consequences and those consequences had consequences. To do whatever I wanted was not an option I'd ever had.

"You've never liked her," I said.

"I never liked how much you liked her. She isn't our mom."

"I know that. But she helped us when—"

Zilla turned to face me, the fire flickering in her eyes. "Did she though? She's richer than god, but instead of, I don't know, loaning you money for school. Loaning me money for Belhaven. Instead of—"

I tried. I really did try not to scoff, but a sound came out of my throat anyway.

"She married you off." She spat the words at me.

"That's not true," I said. "And you can't be angry because she didn't just give us money. We had no right to expect that."

"She married you off," Zilla said again. Each word a bullet, and I tried not to flinch. "To a guy who hurt you. And she knew he was doing it, didn't she?"

I felt myself go still. The lie too slow to my lips.

"I knew it," she said and stood up. "She knew and let me guess . . . She sent you back to him? Tell me, Poppy. How exactly did she help you?"

"She helped you!" I cried, getting to my feet.

Yes. Of course, I'd wondered when Caroline suggested it, why I had to marry the senator. Why she couldn't help me get a job. Or yes, even loan us the money. But those weren't solutions to the problem of Belhaven and the banks.

"Don't," Zilla said. "Don't do that. Don't hide behind me. She manipulated you."

"Manipulated?" I cried. "You're safe. I'm safe. We're . . . fucking rich, Zilla."

"Don't pretend like you care about the money."

"Don't pretend like the money doesn't help us!"

Maybe it was the reflection of the fire, but my sister's eyes were wild. "The money. This—" she looked over my head at the house behind me, "—it's a fucking jail. And you know it. She put you in jail."

"Why? Why would she do that? Do you hear yourself, Zilla?"

She sighed heavily through her nose. "I'm clear. I'm on my meds. I'm fine. I'm just finally telling you what I've thought for a long time. Which is . . . Caroline is using you for something. I don't know what."

Paranoid delusions. Zilla's specialty.

I stood up. "I'm exhausted, and I'm going to bed. You're welcome to stay. But put the fire out before you come to bed."

CHAPTER FOURTEEN

I WAS DREAMING of my 8th grade graduation trip. We went skiing. I hated skiing, but I loved sitting by fireplaces reading books, so while my classmates were all mastering the bunny hill and making out on the ski lift, I was curled up in the corner of the lodge reading a stolen and very forbidden copy of *Flowers in the Attic*. It was just getting good, and by good, I mean *awful*, when someone sat down in the comfy chair next to mine. Black shoes were kicked up on the ottoman next to my Otto the Snowman Socks.

"Hello, Poppy."

"Ronan!" I smiled at him. "What are you doing here?"

"You're here." He shrugged beneath the fine white fabric of his shirt. He had that 'I've been working hard' look about him that was one of my favorite looks. His hair fell down over his eyes, and he swept it up off his face.

"You're handsome," I told him.

"I know. I fuck so many women."

"You don't fuck me."

"Because you're a little girl."

"I liked it when you kissed me."

"That won't happen again," he said with a laugh. "I don't make a habit of kissing girls like you."

Girls like me.

"The fire is big," he said.

"I know. I like it." I turned to look at the fireplace, but it was cold. Empty. But the smell of smoke was still sharp in the air. "What's happening?" I asked Ronan.

"Wake up, little girl!" He leaned forward, his nose almost brushing mine. "Wake up!"

The smoke was real. And I went from waking and baffled to up and out of my bed in a heart beat. The air was hazy with smoke coming in my cracked open French doors.

I hung my head, limp with relief. Zilla must still be out there with the fire. I crossed the room and snapped back the curtain. I pushed open the French door the rest of the way and realized it wasn't just a fire in the fire pit. My whole back yard was on fire. Literally on fire. Yellow flames engulfed the fence around my shower, the bushes at the deep end of the pool were incinerated.

I raced down the hallway and pounded on the door of my sister's room. There was no answer, so I ran in and found her, sleeping like she always did, kitty corner across the bed, the sheets in a knot around her legs.

"Zilla!"

She woke up with a start. "What? What's . . ."

"You didn't put the fire out. We have to go."

"Fire?" Her hair was sticking up in a wild rooster tail over the back of her head, and I wanted to kill her and hug her all at the same time.

How, I wondered, could she do this to me?

I grabbed her by the wrist like she was a little girl and yanked her out of the bed. Furious and scared.

"Oh my god," she said. "That's smoke."

"Yeah, Zilla. You didn't put out the fire."

"I did. I swear . . . Poppy, listen. I did. I put it out."

"Clearly not." We ran down the stairs into the kitchen. Outside the sliding glass doors, it was a wall of flame. Red and orange, licking at the bright black sky. It was so hot in the kitchen, smoke thick at the ceiling and getting thicker every minute.

And loud. So loud. I remembered the fire in

our childhood home, screaming at Zilla but her not hearing me over the sounds of the fire eating the wood of the house we grew up in.

It was all of that. Again.

"Holy shit," Zilla said, beside me. "I swear I did not do this."

Smoke was coming in through the seam in the patio doors, and I had the feeling that the glass wasn't going to stand all that heat, just as it cracked in one huge catastrophic fission from one corner to the other.

I grabbed my phone from the counter where I charged it every night.

"Go!" I shouted at my sister just as the sound of the house alarm could be heard over the roar of the fire outside and my own internal screaming.

"Poppy?" It was Theo coming in the front door.

Oh my god. The relief was astounding.

"We're here!" I shouted and pushed my sister towards the front door. "We're okay!"

"I called 911!" he shouted. He was standing in the doorway, wearing grey sweatpants and a t-shirt and nothing else. He didn't even have shoes on. "You need to get out of this house!"

I followed Zilla out the door, and Theo grabbed my elbow. "Is there anything you need to grab? Documents? Anything important?"

In case the house burned down before fire trucks could get here. This house had not a single thing in it that I cared about. Not a single thing. I thought of that banker's box from the lawyer, but it was just paperwork.

"No," I told him.

He nodded, like he understood and put his arm over my shoulder, and we ran out into the lane. It felt like years, but it was probably only a few minutes before we heard the sirens.

"Poppy," Zilla said. She stood in front of me with red-rimmed eyes and wild hair. "I swear to you, I put out the fire."

Some things are worth the consequences. She said that earlier tonight. As well as all the shit about Caroline and how the house was a prison.

"You don't believe me?" she asked, and she didn't sound angry. She sounded hurt. She looked hurt.

"I don't know what to believe," I told her honestly. Tears from the smoke and from my baffled heart and our bruised past welled up in my eyes.

Zilla licked her lips, tears in her eyes too. "I know . . . I mean, I guess I understand that I deserve that in some capacity. But you know I'm good right now. I'm on my meds. I'm stable. I'm going to fucking nursing school, Pops. I'm not a person who burns down houses anymore."

The sirens were no longer in the distance. They were deafening as the trucks made their way into my little cul-de-sac. Theo herded us out of the way.

"They'll have questions for you," he said to me.

"I don't have any answers."

Over my shoulder his arm tightened. A strange hug, and I leaned into him. A strange hug back. And then he stepped forward to go talk to the firefighters pouring out of the trucks, and I was so grateful that he was going to answer questions, because I was terrified of the answers I had.

"Poppy?" Ronan's accent pulled me away from my sister. I took a step to the side to find him standing in the shadows. His face all pale angles in the gloom.

"What are you doing here?" I asked, astounded to see him. He was dressed in a dark overcoat with black gloves on his hands. He smelled of smoke, though I imagine the whole neighborhood did.

"I heard the sirens."

"It's four in the morning."

He didn't answer. "Are you all right?"

"Fine. I'm—" I stepped towards him, and he eased deeper into the shadows, his eyes flicking over my shoulder. I turned and saw Theo standing there. Nondescript but steady Theo with all the worry in his eyes.

What was wrong with me that my internal compass led me constantly to the cruel man in the shadows instead of the steadfast man right there in front of me?

"Poppy," Theo said. "The fire chief has some questions for you."

"Yeah. I'm coming." I turned but Ronan was gone.

But his words from earlier remained.

Don't trust anyone.

And why was he here? So conveniently at 4 am?

The sun was coming up over the hill behind me when the fire was finally out. It had spread to the kitchen, and the investigators were combing through the wreckage.

"Do you have some place to go?" The fire chief asked me. "We won't have answers until later today, and you've been standing out here for hours."

"We can go to my apartment," Zilla said.

"That's so far away." And frankly that it was exactly what Zilla wanted me to do earlier in the night did nothing to ease my fear that she'd had something to do with this fire as a means to the end she craved. As long as her scales of justice were balanced, damn the consequences.

"You can stay at the cottage," Theo said. "I'll leave."

"I'm not kicking you out of your house."

"Then where will you go?" Zilla asked.

"A hotel in town," I said. "I need to be close in case the fire chief has more questions."

"That's why god created cell phones," Zilla said.

"Please, Zilla," I said in a low murmur.

"I'll go with you—"

I shook my head, and she didn't fight me. Which actually only made me more worried she had a guilty conscience.

Why would she keep the fire going and then go to sleep? She's homicidal. Not suicidal. And, I really didn't think she wanted me hurt in any way. She just wanted me free of the senator and his world.

But when Zilla was in justice mode she didn't always connect the dots. She acted on instinct and maybe . . . maybe her instincts just led her to this outrageous and dangerous action.

"Just go," I told her. "Go home. I'll be in touch."

"Pops?" she breathed, and I heard all her regret. All her sorrow. But I could not manage it on top of my own.

Her car was in the long driveway, and I stood in the road until she drove by, her hand lifted and pressed to the glass.

"Poppy?" It was Theo.

"You've been so good to me tonight, Theo. Head on home, would you?"

"Where are you going to go?"

"I'm going to stay at a hotel."

"I'll drive you."

I shook my head. "I think I need the walk."

And after giving my cell phone information to absolutely everyone who needed it, I turned and walked to the end of my cul de sac, onto the small trail through the woods, up over the hill. On the other side, I broke through the treeline into the tall grass, and to my shock, I saw someone coming down the hill from the Constantine Compound. A woman. And when she saw me, she started running.

The sob I'd been holding in burst out of my

chest, and I went running to meet her.

Caroline threw her arms around me and ab-sorbed my impact.

"Ronan just told me," she said. She was in silk pajamas with an overcoat thrown over her shoulders. Her feet were stuffed into Hunter boots. I saw in my mind what must have happened. She came downstairs for coffee and the newspaper only to find Ronan there, unreadable with news of the fire.

And she came running.

This was the part of Caroline that Zilla never understood. Never got to see.

"Are you all right?" she asked, cupping my face.

"Fine. We got out before the fire spread to the house."

"We?"

"Zilla was there."

"Where is she now?"

"I sent her back to the city. She . . ." I wasn't going to put my suspicion into words. And with one look at Caroline's face I saw that she understood.

"Do you know that for sure?"

"No," I said quickly. And even managing to laugh, like—oh my god, how silly we are to even be talking about this.

"But it does feel like . . . something she might do?"

To that I had no answer, and the weight of the evening rested on my neck and on my heart. I hung my head.

"Okay. You're here." She turned us towards the compound, and together we started walking across the grass. "You're safe. For as long as you need."

THERE WAS COFFEE and scrambled eggs. Granola and fresh fruit, but I couldn't sit down.

"I smell like smoke," I said, sniffing my hair.

"Of course. Denise will show you to your room," Caroline said, squeezing me one last time. She'd had her arm around my shoulder the whole walk up the hill to the house, and she'd kept it there through the house. The support was wonderful.

But I hadn't had so much in so long, it was almost too much.

I followed Denise through the house upstairs to the wing of guest rooms. She stopped in front of the furthest door. "This one is the most private," she said.

"Thank you."

"There are towels and a robe in the bathroom. Would you like me to send someone to get clothes?"

Everything at my house smelled like smoke. Or was ruined by the water from the hoses. I shook my head. "I'll handle everything later." That seemed like a good answer even though it was pure bullshit. Denise nodded and walked back down the hallway. Morning sunlight came in through the bay windows, illuminating everything.

The bedroom was cream and pale blue, the bed a raft of comforters and pillows. A monument to sleep. I pulled the blinds and the room went dark, and the exhaustion filled me up from my toes to the top of my head.

Shower. Shower and then sleep and then . . . well, whatever comes next, I suppose.

I washed my hair three times and scrubbed the top layer of skin off my body in a hope that I could get the smell off and the fear. The fear that my sister was coming unhinged again. Fear that Ronan had done this to scare me away. Fear. Fear. Fear.

What in the world would vanquish this fear? What mantra could I recite? What research could I do? How could I pluck this like a cancer right out of my head, so I could sleep? So I could plan and think of what to do next?

Part of me wanted to let Caroline handle this, the way she'd handled my life when it fell apart last time. But as soon as I thought it, put it into concrete terms, I recoiled.

I'd spent the last two years letting fear rule my life. Letting it shove me in corners and walk in the shadows hoping to be unnoticed. Not again. Not ever again.

If anyone was going to save me this time, it was me. It had to be.

Wrapped in a pink silk robe, my hair in a towel, I walked into the dark bedroom comforted slightly by my determination. I wasn't sure how I would do any of this, but believing was half the battle. Or so I'd been told.

Perhaps it would all be easier once I got some sleep.

There was a quiet knock on the door and expecting Denise, I said, "Come in."

Only to have the door slide open and reveal the one thing, the one person who could put a pin in all my bravery and who, at the same time, made me ache for the things I wanted to be brave enough for.

Ronan.

CHAPTER FIFTEEN

"**A**RE YOU ALL right?" he asked, stepping into the room. He shut the door behind him, and a liquid thrill and a liquid fear seeped through all my exhaustion, and I was suddenly wide awake.

Suddenly very aware of this thin robe clinging to my damp skin.

"Fine. What are you doing here?" There was no way Caroline would approve of her pet fixer being in this room with me.

He glanced away at the dim window, his hands in the pockets of his dark pants. His silence was deafening, and I realized he wasn't entirely sure.

"Did you start that fire?"

His eyes met mine, and I saw deep . . . fear. For me. And I was small and tired and he'd crushed me every time we were together, so I had no reason to feel emboldened by that look in his eye, but I did.

"No," he said. "But the investigator said it wasn't an accident."

"What? How do you know that before me?"

"Because I had something he wanted enough that he broke the rules and gave me what I wanted. That's how it works, Princess."

"What did you have?"

"It doesn't matter."

"How can you say that? Of course—"

"His throat, Poppy. I had his throat in my hand, and if he didn't tell me what I wanted to know I was going to kill him."

I shut my mouth so fast my teeth clicked.

He stepped closer to me. "What matters is that the fire in the fire pit had been put out. It didn't spread. They found accelerant all over the outside of the house. It was intentional. The fire was supposed to scare you or kill you."

I sat down hard on the edge of the bed. Between the comforter and my robe, I nearly slid right off, but Ronan reached out and caught me.

"My sister wouldn't do that," I said.

"Well, maybe the fire was supposed to kill your sister."

"Why? None of this makes sense."

"I know." He sat down beside me.

There was a long simple moment of silence

between us as we sat shoulder to shoulder on that bed. And I was exhausted and scared and really what I wanted in that moment more than anything was comfort. From him. Which was like hoping a knife would wrap its arms around you, but I was somewhere near rock bottom when it came to my mental and emotional reserves.

"Why did you kiss me?" I asked. "In my office. You said you wouldn't kiss me and then—"

"I break all my rules around you, Poppy. Every single one."

"No kissing is a rule?"

He nodded, staring down at his hands.

"What other rules do you break?"

He sighed, rubbed at his face. The silence stretched and stretched, and I was sure he was never going to answer me. And if he couldn't answer even one of my questions then what was the point of him? Us. I opened my mouth to tell him to go, to let me rest. To leave me alone.

But then he started to talk. "When I was a kid, Da got us a place in social housing. A shit bag flat. Leaky roof. Gangs, fucking everywhere. Every corner," he said.

And I sat so still. So quiet. Terrified if I moved or said something, he might walk away.

"School was miles away, like. And I was saving

up money running errands for some of the old folks around so I could get a skateboard." He took a deep breath and let it out real slow. "Just so I could get to school. But my Da kept finding the money, and I'd have to start all over. And then this family moves in next door. And there's a kid my age and I'm like . . . crazy with happiness. I'm like on his step at dawn looking for this kid."

His smile broke my heart. Broke it right in half.

"And his family wasn't too happy with him hanging out with the likes of me, but we got on all right. And then it's the boy's birthday, and he gets a new skateboard and he gives me his old one. And I reckon I lose my mind I'm so happy and I . . . show it to my Da. Which, I honestly, don't know what I was thinking. But he grabs the skateboard, and it was just cheap plywood over some shit wheels but he smashes it over my shoulder. Breaks it into two pieces, dislocates my shoulder, and then he grabs me and the two skateboard pieces and we go outside where my friend is playing with his new board in the street, and my Da pushes the kid off the board, picks it up and smashes his skateboard on the ground."

"Why?" I asked. "Why would he do that?"

"Well. The best I could figure being just a kid

and with a dislocated shoulder and all, was that I couldn't be happy. I couldn't have the skateboard, and I couldn't have a friend. The boy never talked to me again."

"Ronan," I sighed, aching with sympathy.

"If I gave my Da even the slightest idea that I liked something, he'd ruin it. And I thought for awhile, I could hide it. Hide what I wanted. So he'd never know." He shook his head. "But I wasn't very good at hiding anything."

"How old were you?"

"Seven."

"You were just a boy."

"Well, I was boy who learned that the best way to not have the things he wanted broken or stolen or thrown in the trash was to not want anything."

"And that . . . that was a rule?"

"I'm twenty-seven years old, Poppy. I've lived by that rule for almost twenty years. And then you came along with your fucking eyes, that spirit I watched get put away and then start to come back out again, it was like watching—" he shook his head, "—spring. It was like watching those little stupid flowers that put their heads up through the frost."

"Are you calling me stupid?"

"So fucking stupid."

"Ronan—"

"But not as fucking stupid as me. Because you're going to get hurt, I know you are. I know it. And the only thing that can save you is you leaving."

"Did you set the fire?" I asked. "To scare me off?"

"No. I mean, I thought it, but I didn't do it."

"Why not?"

"Because I don't—" He stopped shook his head and got to his feet, like he was going to leave.

I grabbed his hand, his fingers curled into a hard fist, like armor against me. "You don't what?"

"Want you to leave."

I stood up, his hand still in mine. My thumb traced the scar on his wrist. "I'm not leaving," I said.

"Cos you're a fucking fool."

"Probably. But there's something here I want too."

He was shaking his head. He yanked his hands free of mine and grabbed my shoulders, lifting me off my feet so I was nearly eye to eye with him. It hurt, his grip on my body. But when everything hurt, you took the pain that had the greatest chance of turning into pleasure.

"You don't want me. You want the way I make you feel."

"I want all of it."

"I haven't even fucked you," he said, like I was pathetic. And I knew what he was doing. Maybe I'd always known. But he was trying to hurt me so I'd stay away.

"We could change that," I whispered. "Right now. You could put your cock—"

"Shut up," he said.

"Inside of me."

He was rigid. His eyes someplace over my head, and I felt every ounce of control he was using to keep himself from doing what he wanted. I stepped back, away. Pulling the tie of my robe as I went. It slid open, revealing my body. My skin soft and pink from the shower. "It's never felt good before. But it would with you, wouldn't it? With us?"

"You think I won't hurt you?"

"You will. But you'll make it feel so good, too. That's what you do to me."

His eyes on me burned. Like the hottest part of the flame, and it hurt. Everything about him hurt. But god, I loved this pain.

"You could fuck me," I said, lying back on the bed. My heels on the edge of the mattress. I parted my legs, slipped my hand down over my pussy. "Right here." I jumped at the brush of my finger over my clitoris. How, I wondered, could I be so tired? So scared? And still want him so much? The world could be coming down around me, and I would still want him. "I could make you feel good, too. The way it's supposed to be."

He came to stand at the foot of the bed between my legs. I held my breath waiting for his touch. And when it came, his hand on my knee, I flinched with the pleasure.

"When did you get so bold?" he asked.

"You made me this way." I dipped a finger deeper inside myself, and he made a sound from his throat, a groan that made me catch my breath. This was some kind of magic between us. We were combustible, and the other held the match.

"You . . . make me want things I can't have, Poppy." His voice sounded final. Cold. Like he was halfway out the door. "I won't fuck you. But I'll make you feel good."

"No." I pushed myself up to sitting. "I don't want that. I don't want—"

He kissed me. So sweet, his lips against mine. I opened my mouth to gasp, to breathe, to have more of him. As much of him as he'd let me, and one hand came up to hold my jaw, the other cupped my breast, squeezing my nipple between his hand and his thumb. I groaned into his mouth.

His mouth was a seduction. Long slow kisses. They never stopped. They rolled one into the other. His tongue against mine. He caught my lower lip with his teeth and pulled until I whimpered. It was too much and not enough all at the same time.

"Ronan," I whimpered, and he pulled away. The kissing over, but he still held my jaw. His eyes on mine.

"You're fucking killing me, Poppy."

"Then we're dying together. I've never . . . I've never felt this way."

He said something, his accent so thick and guttural I couldn't understand it. He pushed me back on the bed. His hand slipped between my legs, and his mouth captured my nipple. I saw stars behind my eyelids, and my hands memorized the feel of his shoulders under his shirt. They were wide and strong, and I clutched them as if I could claim him. As if wanting him so badly I was crazed with it, would grant me the right to call him mine. The way I wanted to call him mine.

And the way I wanted to be his.

"Fuck me," I breathed. "Please."

"No, Poppy. I won't. You're not for me. You'll regret even letting me touch you this much." He shifted like he was going to pull away. Like he was going to stop.

"Ronan."

He groaned and pressed the top of his head to my chest and shifted his body so my legs were pressed out wide. "You'll only get fucking hurt if you keep on like this, Poppy," he said, but his words barely made any sense. His fingers were inside me, and my body was made out of sugar and light and I was losing my grip on everything except him. Everything except how he made me feel.

I grabbed his wrist, keeping him close, and I exploded into a thousand ecstatic pieces. And when I came back together, I was different. Different each time he touched me. He was standing up, moving away. His eyes already shuttered. His thoughts and feelings behind glass.

I grabbed him by the belt, felt the hard press of his cock against the heel of my hand and pressed against it until he groaned. His head thrown back. I was so quick he didn't have a chance to stop me. To pull against me or push me away. His belt was undone, and I slipped my hand into his pants, catching the hard length of him through his underwear.

But the reality was, I had no idea what to do with him. How to . . . make him feel good the way he did me. He was a man, a dangerous man, with a past I didn't understand or know. And I was just this foolish flower, sticking my head out of the snow despite knowing I'd be hurt by what I wanted most.

"Show me," I whispered, coming to the edge of the bed. Stroking him, squeezing him. "Show me what you like."

Again, he said something I couldn't understand, but with one hand he shoved his underwear out of the way revealing his cock, and his other hand cupped me behind the neck and pulled me to him.

"Open your goddamn mouth," he growled, and I did. His cock slipping past my lips. I had done this once before. Damon in the library. And he'd been so nervous and sweet, and he kept asking me if I was all right.

Ronan wasn't going to ask me that at all. He didn't care. He had lost control and was using me. And all I could do was brace my hands against his hips as he fucked into my mouth. Long and slow.

Faster.

I loved every fucking second.

And then suddenly, he pulled out, his hands still holding my neck. His head bowed so I couldn't see his face. Panting, aching, I waited for him to continue or to say something. I leaned forward but he held me still.

I felt all of my inexperience. Every night in that bed with the senator, unmoved and just wanting it to be over. Those fumbling sweet moments with Damon who smelled like books and weed. What did I know, what could I possibly know about pleasing this man?

"I'm sorry," I whispered.

"For what?"

"For not . . . being what you want?" That made him look at me, not that it mattered. He looked so angry. "For not knowing how to do this."

"If I could—" He stopped himself, looked at the ceiling. I looked down, wrapping my robe around my naked body. If he could go back, he'd never have talked to me at that party. Or taken me into the room at the gala. If he could do it all over again, it would never be with me.

"Stop," he said.

"I think—"

He squeezed my neck, and my eyes flew to his. "Open your mouth for me," he whispered, and he was smiling. Actually smiling. So, stunned, I did what he asked, and he eased forward, slipping his cock back between my lips. He was salty. Wet. Come, I realized. And so hard. Hard against my lips. The back of my throat. And now, now he was looking right at me, and I was looking at him, and I'd never in my life been so connected to someone. So vulnerable and naked.

"Look at you." He kept breathing like he'd stumbled onto something beautiful and mystifying, and no one had ever talked to me like that. The head of his cock hitting the back of my throat and it was . . . I couldn't breathe. But I didn't want him to stop.

He pulled away, and I moaned, licking him as he slipped out of my mouth. He stopped, like he might actually walk away. And there'd been too much of that. I put my arm around his hips, pulling him back to me, sucking him down even as it seemed he hesitated.

"I can't . . . fuck. Jesus. Poppy," he groaned, and then I felt him surrender. He cradled my face in his hands and shook, coming in my mouth.

It was oddly quiet. And almost holy. He trembled against me, his head bowed, lips moving as if praying, and I languished in it. Reveled in it. His surrender, and ease. The power and communion of touching him like this. Making him feel like this.

I could not ever love this man. It would be stupid beyond even my capabilities. Signing myself up for a pain not even I could imagine. But this intimacy. His slow withdrawal from my mouth. His taste on my tongue. His fingers twitching in my hair. This pinpoint of pain in my heart.

It was a revelation.

"I've never felt this way before," I said.

"It's sex," he said.

"I'd feel this for anyone who touched me the way you do?"

He stepped back, tucking himself away. Jerking his clothes back into place when he finally looked at me, he was the stranger I'd grown used to. Everything hidden. Everything gone.

With the senator, I learned self-preservation so well. I was a master. So good in fact, I was barely living. But with this man, I kept throwing myself against his spikes and his stone-face.

He is only going to hurt me.

Suddenly I was exhausted. Down to my bones.

There was no way to hold up my chin. No way to straighten my shoulders for one more cruel word. One more beautiful touch.

"Come on," he said, helping me into the bed, pulling out the quilt from under my body and tucking me in. His fingers—perhaps by accident, I couldn't be sure, I couldn't be sure of anything with this man—brushed my cheek.

"How am I supposed to survive you?" I asked.

"You're not," he said.

CHAPTER SIXTEEN

I WOKE UP to a dark sky. The day gone. Feeling stoned—not that I'd ever been stoned, which actually at this moment in my life seemed criminal. I was a twenty-two-year-old. How had I never gotten high?

I'd learned how to drive; maybe smoking a joint would be next.

Starving, wrapped in the pink silk robe, I wandered downstairs looking for a cup of coffee and my cell phone.

Instead, I found Caroline in the kitchen's breakfast nook, a glass of wine and an open manila folder in front of her. Behind her the sky was indigo. The dark shadow of trees taking bites out of the slightly lighter blue. The lamp over the table was glass and gold fixtures, and cast angular shadows over Caroline's face.

She wore a pair of yoga pants and a cashmere sweater. Her feet were bare. I'd never seen her so . . . undone. She looked somehow even younger. More beautiful.

"Hey," I said.

"You're awake," she said with the kind of smile that always felt motherly to me.

"Finally."

"You want a glass of wine?"

"No, but could I get some coffee?"

"I can get Denise to make it."

"I got it—"

I turned to find Ronan leaning against the counter, blending into the shadows. His feet crossed at the ankles. His white shirt pulled taut over his shoulders. I realized I had not ever seen his body. He'd seen me naked and crying. And he'd only been dressed and distant.

"Oh," I said, my face suddenly hot. My nipples beneath the robe, hard. "I don't mean to interrupt. I can leave."

"No. You're not interrupting anything," Caroline said. "Well, you are, but . . . it concerns you."

"Me?" I turned, coffee forgotten.

"Come sit," she said, patting the spot at the wooden table across from her. I slid across the bench seat, and she handed me the folder.

"What is this?"

"Something I wasn't going to talk to you

about. But, after last night and the fire, I think . . . I think we need to talk about it."

I opened the folder.

"Oh my god," I breathed, looking out the window, trying to blink away the image of my husband, bone white with a black and red hole in the middle of his head.

"Sorry," Caroline said. "I should have warned you."

"What is this?" I asked, still not looking at the image.

"I hired a private coroner," Caroline said.

"It was suicide, why would you hire a coroner?"

"Because the Bishop's Landing coroner has ties to the Morelli family. Ulrich—he's our private investigator, you know—suggested it after getting wind of possible Morelli involvement."

"The Morellis?" It was like she was speaking French. And she had a private investigator and coroner on call? "What . . . what do they have to do with anything?"

"Your husband and I were working together on several issues," Caroline said. "And many of those issues worked in opposition to the Morellis' plans."

"Plans for what?"

"Listen to me, Poppy." Caroline was talking to me like I was a kindergartner which I resented but also probably needed. My brain was on fire. "Your husband had plenty of enemies. But I didn't trust the coroner's report, because of the Morelli connection. That's why I hired a private coroner."

Ronan set a cup of coffee at my elbow, and I jumped so high I nearly smacked it out of his hand.

Caroline reached over and opened the file again. I closed my eyes.

"Poppy. You can't close your eyes against this. Jim's gunshot wasn't self-inflicted."

I gaped at her. Laughed, incredulously. I was still dreaming. I had to be. "You're saying someone else shot him?"

"That's what the coroner report says. Someone shot him and tried to make it look like a suicide."

"He's a US senator," I cried. "That's . . . that's an outrageous cover up."

"I know."

Ronan faded back into the shadows, but I was aware of him there. In the room. A magnet I could not ignore and felt myself bending towards, despite knowing I would get hurt. Despite knowing he did not want me bending towards him.

"How?" I cried. "How could someone cover that up?"

"The Morellis have a lot of power," Caroline said. "And it all starts with the crime scene and with the original falsified coroner report. And with your statement."

"My statement?"

"You told the police he'd been acting strange. Not sleeping. Home more than in the office. Combined with a falsified doctor's report—"

"The doctor lied?" I asked.

"People will do anything for the right amount of money."

"But why?"

"That's not what's important right now, Poppy," she said.

"Not important?" I cried. "Am I still sleeping? Is this like . . . a stress dream?"

"Between your husband being murdered and the fire at your house; I fear that someone might be trying to hurt you, Poppy," Caroline said.

"But why?" I was literally NO ONE. Hurting me, killing me would have no impact on the world. None whatsoever.

Caroline pushed her wine glass away and

grabbed my hand. "Your sister—"

I jerked my hand back. "No."

"You can't tell me you haven't thought it."

"She wouldn't hurt me. Zilla wouldn't hurt me. I mean, killing the senator, maybe . . . if she was in one of her manic phases. But covering it up like that? She doesn't have that kind of power." I stood up. Frantic and strange in my body. Two families had that kind of power—the Morellis and the Constantines. "How do they know he was killed by someone else? The coroner you hired, what did he find out that the other guy lied about?"

"The angle of the bullet through his skull." Caroline said. "No residue on his hands."

"This can't be true."

"It's true, Poppy," Ronan said. I whirled to face him, and his stillness was not threatening in this moment. It was a comfort. A rock in a storm. "It's true."

"What about the medical records. The cancer?"

"The doctor who signed the paperwork is gone."

"Gone?"

"He's just . . . vanished."

Oh god. Officially this was too much. Officially, the room and my world were spinning.

"So," I said. "What you're saying is that someone killed my husband. Made it look like a suicide. Bribed a doctor?" I shrugged, manically. "Killed a doctor? And the coroner was somehow in on it, and now they want to kill me?"

"Please, calm down, Poppy," Caroline said.

"And I'm supposed to believe you?"

"Of course," she said calmly. "Of course you are supposed to believe me. I have only ever had your best interests at heart."

"Which is why you married me off to Jim. Right? All part of my best interests?"

It was like the room cracked. Or my brain? Was it my brain cracking?

Caroline sat up straight. God, she looked like a queen. Regal even in her bare feet. No one ever doubted her.

Except Zilla and now, apparently me.

"He was looking for a wife, and you needed money," Caroline said.

"A wife. Hilarious. He was looking for someone he could hurt with impunity. And you gave me to him."

"You sound like your sister," Caroline said.

"Maybe I should have listened to her more."

"Right. When she was restrained at Belhaven.

After she burned down your childhood home. After she went after that priest? Who made all that go away? Hmmm?" Caroline asked. "When you talk about listening to your sister, who kept her out of jail?"

"You did," I whispered. And I let my gratitude for that carry me into whatever she asked of me. I looked at Ronan who was standing to the side, arms at his sides like he could grab me and wrap me in a strait jacket if he needed to. "I'm going to go home," I said.

"I know you're upset," Caroline said. "But I don't know if that's a good idea."

"I know. It is a good idea. It's a great idea. It is in fact the only idea." I walked out of the kitchen towards the front door, walking down hallways past rooms filled with bad memories. "Where is my phone? I just need my phone and maybe some shoes?"

"Poppy, you are being ridiculous," Caroline said.

Sure. Yep. Probably. But I wasn't exactly sure what else there was to do in this situation. I needed some distance. A chance to think. A goddamn cup of coffee.

Denise arrived from some dark hallway. "Do you need some help?" she asked, her eyes taking in everyone.

"Shoes, Denise. Any shoes will do. And my phone."

Denise looked back at Caroline as if to get permission. "Look at me!" I barked. "Talk to me. I want my shoes and my phone."

Denise vanished for a second and came back with the boots I'd worn last night and my phone, which was of course dead. "The clothes are still in the wash. They smelled of smoke."

"This is great." I shoved my feet in the boots and grabbed my dead phone from her. "Perfect."

I was out the front door before I realized Ronan was behind me. "I don't need—"

"I'm driving you," he said.

"I—"

"I'm driving you."

We walked down the front walk, around to the side of the house where there were a few cars parked. One of them a sleek black sports car. "Get in."

"Are you mad?"

"Get in the car."

I slipped in the passenger side as Ronan got in behind the wheel. The engine started with a roar, and we took off so fast my head hit the headrest.

"Why are *you* mad?" I cried.

"I'm not." He shifted gears like we were in some kind of car race, and I grabbed the seat belt, slipping it over my body.

"You just always drive like you're behind in the Indy 500?"

His lips twitched like he wanted to laugh.

"Was all of that true?" I asked. "Someone killed the senator?"

"Yes."

We rolled to a stop at the bottom of the hill. If we turned right, we would head down to the highway. Left we went up to my house. He didn't turn the car. He didn't press on the gas.

"I'm that way," I said, pointing left.

"I can take you anywhere," he said. "Right now. Any place away from here."

He wasn't looking at me and it wasn't . . . romantic. It wasn't about me and him. It was about the Constantines and the Morellis. It was about Caroline and being clever.

I realized with a sinking heart that maybe everything, every moment between us was about Caroline and being clever.

Motherfucker.

"I need to go home," I said. "Frankly, I don't know if any of this is true."

"The fire chief—"

"Talked to you? And not me? That's convenient."

"You think I'm lying? You think Caroline is lying?"

"I think I'm being manipulated. You talk to the fire chief; she has some private coroner. Suddenly every terrible thing that's happened to me is about the Constantine and Morelli feud. I mean . . . listen to how ridiculous all that sounds."

"Call the fire chief."

"I will. When I'm home. When I've had a goddamn cup of coffee."

"You can't stay there, Poppy. It's reckless. Stupid. You could—"

"I know!" I shouted. "I know I can't stay there and I won't. Okay. I won't stay. But my stuff is there. My . . ." I looked down at my dead phone. "My phone charger. My purse. Money. I need to get organized to leave. I can't just vanish."

He turned and looked at me. Really looked at me. And my mouth was dry and my anger fizzed and popped but so did everything else I felt for him.

"There's something going on," he said. "Something . . . I don't know about. And I know about everything. *Everything*, Poppy."

"You mean the fire?"

He glanced away, to the right and the highway past it. And for a second I thought he was going to ignore what I was saying and drive me away. I put my hand on the door handle, thinking I would run before I'd let him take me away.

"I don't know if the fire was to hurt you or warn Caroline or destroy something."

"Destroy what?" I asked. "The house doesn't have—" Oh. The paperwork from the lawyer? That would be . . . ridiculous.

"What?" he asked. "What are you thinking?"

"Nothing," I lied. "I'm not thinking anything. Just take me home," I said.

He turned left and gunned the engine.

The front of my house was covered in yellow tape. There were black scorch marks on the side of the house. Half the trees were blackened sticks. It was so much worse than I thought. So much more real.

Ronan sat, stone still, eyes on the house.

"I'd invite you in," I said with a laugh. "But—"

"Go," he said, like he was just so done with me.

All-righty. Carefully trying not to show him any part of myself beneath the robe, which was ridiculous when I'd already shown him so much, I opened the door. "I suppose I'll see you," I said. "Lurking in the shadows somewhere."

"Just be careful," he said, and when he looked at me, the words dried up in my mouth. Anger, such pure anger it was like being frozen in place, radiated off him.

"Goodbye," I whispered and got out of that car. Away from him with as much of myself as possible. God, when would I learn to stop giving men pieces of me just because they wanted them? I ran to the front door of my house, which had been unlocked after all the drama of the night. The floor inside was wet and sooty. Muddy.

I followed the cold draft coming in the back of the house from the kitchen.

"Oh my god," I breathed. The glass was shattered from the sliding glass door and shards of it were blown all around the kitchen. More yellow tape fluttered in the breeze on the patio outside.

I looked at all this damage. The absolute ruin of my house and wondered . . . why I didn't care. My cage was finally destroyed.

I pulled my dead phone out of the pocket of my silk robe and plugged it into my charger sitting on the counter like nothing had happened.

They'd turned the gas last night in an effort to prevent my home from going up like a bomb. But my electricity was still on, and my little coffee pot was working and so was my fridge. Within a few minutes I had a hot cup of coffee with milk. And in the closet, I found my sweatshirt and put that on over my robe. The phone was going to take a few more minutes so I found myself standing in front of the door that led to Jim's office.

The night he died . . . killed himself? Was murdered? The gunshot woke me up, and I lay in bed for a long time, freaking out and scared. Expecting, any minute, for the senator to come upstairs and tell me he'd shot an intruder. But the more time that passed I thought maybe I'd been wrong and there wasn't a gunshot. If something was wrong the senator would be sure to let me know. And I fell back to sleep.

I slept until 7 am, went downstairs. Made my coffee. And it wasn't until 8 am when I heard his secretary scream that I knew something awful had happened.

That picture of him in the folder had been taken on a gurney. If there were pictures of him in the library after the shooting, I'd never seen them. I'd never actually seen him. His secretary had had the foresight to throw a blanket over him. All before I even made my way down the hallway.

I'd been grateful all along that I didn't need to look at my dead husband. But now it threw another layer of suspicion over everything. Had I seen him, would I have been able to tell if he'd been murdered?

Not likely. But still.

I stood at the door to Jim's office, the desk in front of it where his poor secretary sat, judging everyone who came to visit. Including me. Especially me. Ugh. I hated her. There was something about that door. The big gold doorknob. The hinges were so big they looked like something out of a medieval prison.

This had been the senator's space, and I'd cared not at all about it.

I didn't want to be in this room then, and I didn't want to be in this room now. I didn't want to believe a word of what Caroline had said. But I had lived with my head in the sand for a long, long time. And it was time to be done.

I had to find some answers for myself.

I pushed open the door to reveal his wood-panelled study. The desk a wide raft that could have held four computers or at least another Jack from *Titanic*. The walls were floor-to-ceiling bookcases. Full of . . . I didn't even know. I never even cared. There was a fireplace and two chairs pulled up in front of it. A drink cart beside it. I wondered who ever sat with him in front of that fire. Because it certainly had never been me.

Had the Morellis sat there? It actually wasn't hard to imagine. Jim had been evil, and evil men usually liked other evil men.

But where did that leave Caroline? Who'd thrust me into Jim's world.

The box from the lawyer was there behind the desk. He'd said there was paperwork regarding the foundation. And Ronan that night in my bedroom had asked if I'd gone to the Morellis to get answers about the foundation.

I grabbed the box and put it on the desk.

"Poppy?" I jumped at the sound of another voice, and the door was pushed open to reveal Theo.

"Hi!" I said. I grabbed the box and put it back behind the desk, kicking it into the shadows.

"I saw the light on in the house and wasn't sure—"

"It's me."

"You're . . . all right?" he asked with a careful smile.

"Never better," I joked. "You want some coffee?"

"It's nine o'clock at night," he said.

"How about a drink?" I asked, pointing to the senator's drink cart.

"Sure."

"Bourbon?"

I set my coffee mug down on the corner of the desk and walked over to the cart to pour half the bottle into one of the tumblers.

He was leaning against the desk, and I handed him the drink and grabbed my coffee cup by his hip. "Have you talked to the fire marshal?"

"Not yet," I said. "My phone is charging."

I sat down in one of the chairs in front of the cold fireplace and took a sip of my coffee. The heat and caffeine waking me up bit by bit.

"You can't stay here tonight," he said. "It's not safe. The whole back wall is gone, and I don't feel good about the roof."

"I know. You know, considering the fire was mostly outside there is so much damage inside."

"It's the water from the hoses. You're going to go back to Mrs. Constantine's?"

I shook my head, had another sip of coffee. "No."

"You want me to drive you into the city?" he asked.

"Yeah," I said. I needed to call my sister, make some kind of amends. But I'd stay in a hotel in the city. I just needed some space. Some room to try and understand what had happened to me. A chance to go through the box in quiet. "I'll pack a bag, call the fire marshal, and if there aren't any problems I should be ready to go soon."

I said all of that but did not get up from the chair.

He sat down in the chair next to mine. "You all right?"

"You know, I've never really spent much time in this room."

"I understand that."

"Did you know?" I asked. It was a stupid question, really. Of course he knew. "About him? I mean the senator?"

"Know what?"

I stared at him until his cheeks turned pink. "We . . . I mean, some of the staff had an idea. Of what he was like with you."

What he was like with you. That was actually hilarious. I mean as far as euphemisms go that was a real doozy. I laughed into my coffee cup.

"What's so funny?"

"I think my life," I said. "I think it's my life that's funny."

I stood up and felt the room spin around me. I braced myself against the chair. The coffee cup suddenly so heavy in my hand.

"Poppy?"

"I'm sorry . . . I just—" Whoa. Maybe I was tired. Just really tired? There'd been a lot of stress.

"I hated that he hurt you," Theo said. I turned to find him right beside me.

"You and me both." Oh, my mouth was weird. I clenched my teeth and let them go. My lips were so . . . big.

"Poppy." His hands cupped my shoulders and slowly ran down to my elbows, and I felt like I was melting. Right into the ground. Right into him.

I put my hand against his chest, pushing him away. I did not want him to get the wrong idea.

"I hate that I have to hurt you."

"What? I'm sorry . . . I don't feel too good." Hurt me? Was that what he said? Or he hated that the senator hurt me? That made more sense.

He grabbed my hand and yanked me towards the door. I tripped and fell, and he all but dragged me as I tried to get to my feet. "Theo. Please . . . Theo!"

He half-pulled, half-dragged me down the hallway, and everything was tilting. "What is happening?"

"You're fucking shit up."

Yeah. I had a way of doing that. I was grabbing onto the wainscoting, trying to find a way to slow this all down. To get myself upright. To make things make sense. But the world was water around me, and my body wasn't under my control.

"What did you give me?" I asked. He ignored me, and I fought to keep myself present. Aware. Fighting. Keep talking, I thought. If I stopped talking I would pass out, and then I'd be in real trouble. "Where are you taking me?" I asked.

"Where I should have just taken you the second that asshole caught a bullet in his head."

"Did you . . . did you kill the senator?" I asked as he shoved open the door from the office wing into the main part of the house.

But Ronan was there. In a black overcoat and black gloves, holding a gun. Pointed right at us.

The world tilted again as suddenly I was held up against Theo's body, and a gun I didn't know he had was pressed against my forehead.

The world was an acid trip around me, but that gun was very real.

And so was Ronan.

"Rivers," Ronan said. "You're making a mess of this."

Behind my back, Theo was breathing hard,

his heart pounding against my ear.

"Clear out, Byrne. This doesn't concern you."

"It doesn't concern the girl either."

I'm the girl. Theo's arm around my chest was making it hard to breathe and whatever I guess he put in my coffee cup made it even harder.

"Ronan," I panted, terrified.

"Leave the girl and go," Ronan said, ignoring me, his eyes on Theo. "Leave right now. I won't follow you."

Theo laughed. "That's not happening. You're a scary motherfucker, Byrne. But you're not the scariest person who wants this girl."

"Who?" I whispered. "Who wants me?"

"We can get you out of the country," Ronan said to Theo. "No one will know."

"The way you did for the senator?" Theo asked. "You gonna help me disappear with a bullet in my head?"

"What?" I jerked against his hold, trying to strain away from him and towards Ronan as best I could.

"Yeah," Theo said against my ear. "Ask me again. That question about what I did to the senator."

"Did you kill the senator?" I asked, my eyes on Ronan, but he didn't look back. He didn't even look at me like I mattered in this situation.

"I didn't," Theo said and pointed his gun at Ronan. "He did."

"Is that true?" I whispered, and Ronan's silence felt like confirmation.

"It's true," Theo said. "And because that asshole killed the senator, you have to come with me."

"Let her go," Ronan said.

"You know what will happen if I do that," Theo said. "The Morellis want blood. I'd rather they had hers."

The world was spinning, but the thought I grabbed a hold of and hung onto was that neither one of these men were here to help me. Both of them would hurt me.

Theo was edging us down the hallway towards the front door, and my feet tripped us up. He caught himself against the wall, the gun for the moment sliding from me to Ronan who, as I stumbled, was nearly on top of us.

Theo pointed the gun at Ronan's head, and I whimpered, tears suddenly burning in my eyes. Someone was going to die tonight, that becoming obvious even to me.

"Oh, Ronan." Theo laughed. "Do not attempt to play the hero now. Guys like you and me, we mean nothing to them. We're fucking tools. So get out of my way and let me do my job."

"I'm going to throw up," I moaned and, frankly, the spinning world was narrowing, growing black around the edges. Empty in the middle. But this was going to be up to me. And my time was running out. The front door was still open and beyond it the night was completely dark. Without the glass in the sliding door in the kitchen, that door was wide open too. And if I went out that way the garage was closer. I could run, get in the car and drive to the city. To my sister. Could I even drive right now? No. Not likely.

I could run. To the willow tree down by the pond. I could hide in the branches, and she would find me. She would keep me safe. She'd bring me Goldfish crackers and icy cold Cokes and we'd go swimming and everything would be okay.

We would be okay.

I'm sorry, Zilla, I thought. *I'm so sorry I thought you were capable of this. That I thought you would hurt me.*

And she left here thinking the very worst.

I'm sorry. I'm so sorry.

We were pawns in a game we didn't even

understand.

"I swear to you, man, I don't want to kill you," Ronan said to Theo. "Let her go."

Theo shoved me, and I didn't actually trip, but I made a convincing lurch to the ground, and while Theo was off balance, I planted my feet and pushed him as hard as I could. All I had was surprise on my side. And this .0001% chance of catching him off guard. He fell away from me, his arm letting me go. Just enough that I could duck under it and make a run for the front door. But I was an idiot, and he caught himself in time to grab my hair. He yanked me back off my feet, and I slammed into the ground so hard I saw stars. My will to fight, to leave, to get to the willow tree and my sister; to maybe find answers about any of the forces pulling the world apart, dwindled down to nothing.

Right now, it felt easier to let the world just go.

And then suddenly there was Ronan, smashing Theo's entire body against the wall.

"Run!" Someone yelled it. Or maybe it was a voice in my head. My sister manifesting after all these years, and I got to my feet, my feet slipping in the boots. But I charged out of that house.

You're about to run the fifty-yard dash in a

ballgown.

He'd said that. A million years ago.

And he killed my husband. Humiliated me. Lied to me. Saved me? Was that what he was doing, right now? He was kind to me when no one was kind to me. Brought part of me back to life that had been dead for so long. Whatever he was, none of it made sense.

I was at the front door when the sound of a gunshot ripped through the house. I fell to the ground, scraping my elbows and knees, throwing my arms up over my head.

In the silence after the gunshot, I turned, looked behind me.

Ronan, framed in the golden light of the open door, stood over Theo's body. His black overcoat blowing out behind him in the cross breeze from all my broken windows. From my entirely broken life.

He was alive. I felt that somewhere. That he'd been the one to survive in the fight with Theo. That the gunshot was not the end of his life. My heart lifted at the sight of him.

I got slowly to my feet. Stumbling and weak from the drugs in my system. Part of me wanted to walk to him. To that bright square of light. To his arms. But I stood there in the cold night, the frosty grass unmoving.

No. He was not the answer. If I could get to my sister I could figure this out. She'd help me put the pieces together.

Or I could ask Ronan. Just ask him what—

He lifted the gun in his hand. Pointing it at me.

At me.

I turned, running into shadows. My heart screaming for my sister. For all the mistakes I made. For the man I'd given so much of myself to.

I heard the gunshot. Felt a sunfire blast through my shoulder. Fell to the earth where my world went dark.

Thank you for reading RUINED! We hope you loved Ronan's dangerous and emotional story. Find out what happens next in BROKEN.

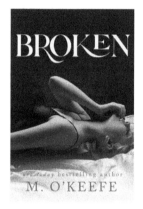

I'm a hunted woman, torn between my past and present, ripped apart by two warring families. Bishop's Landing is no longer safe for us. Ronan hides me in his own corner of the world. A place steeped in sin and shadow. The priests who raised him know his secrets.

If I'm not careful, they could come crashing down on us both. Because Ronan isn't the man I thought he was. He's someone else. An enemy I never saw coming.

You can find BROKEN on Amazon, Barnes & Noble, Apple Books, Kobo and Google Play.

And you can read the story of Winston Constantine, the oldest son in the Constantine family and head of the business empire, story right now!

Money can buy anything. And anyone. As the head of the Constantine family, I'm used to people bowing to my will. Cruel, rigid, unyielding—I'm all those things. When I discover the one woman who doesn't wither under my gaze, but instead smiles right back at me, I'm intrigued.

You can find STROKE OF MIDNIGHT on Amazon, Barnes & Noble, Apple Books, Kobo and Google Play now.

The warring Morelli and Constantine families have enough bad blood to fill an ocean, and their brand new stories will be told by your favorite dangerous romance authors. See what books are available now and sign up to get notified about new releases here...
www.dangerouspress.com

ABOUT THE AUTHOR

Molly O'Keefe has always known she wanted to be a writer (except when she wanted to be a florist or a chef and the brief period of time when she considered being a cowgirl). And once she got her hands on some romances, she knew exactly what she wanted to write.

She published her first Harlequin romance at age 25 and hasn't looked back. She loves exploring every character's road towards happily ever after.

Originally from a small town outside of Chicago, she went to university in St. Louis where she met and fell in love with the editor of her school newspaper. They followed each other around the world for several years and finally got married and settled down in Toronto, Ontario. They welcomed their son into their family in 2006, and their daughter in 2008. When she's not at the park or cleaning up the toy room, Molly is working hard on her next novel, trying to exercise, stalking Tina Fey on the internet and dreaming of the day she can finish a cup of coffee without interruption.

NEWSLETTER
www.molly-okeefe.com

FACEBOOK
facebook.com/MollyOKeefeBooks

INSTAGRAM
instagram.com/mokeefeauthor

About Midnight Dynasty

Midnight Dynasty is a brand new world where enemies and lovers are often one and the same.

JOIN THE FACEBOOK GROUP HERE
www.dangerouspress.com/facebook

FOLLOW US ON INSTAGRAM
www.instagram.com/dangerouspress

SIGN UP FOR THE NEWSLETTER
www.dangerouspress.com

Copyright

Ruined © 2021 by M. O'Keefe
Print Edition

Cover design by Book Beautiful

Ingram Content Group UK Ltd.
Milton Keynes UK
UKHW012245150323
418612UK00004B/241